T0123231

CRY,
the Rich Island

Daniel Michael

authorHOUSE

AuthorHouse™
1663 Liberty Drive
Bloomington, IN 47403
www.authorhouse.com
Phone: 833-262-8899

Published by AuthorHouse 08/10/2023

ISBN: 978-1-6655-6850-0 (sc)
ISBN: 978-1-6655-6851-7 (e)

Library of Congress Control Number: 2022915135

Print information available on the last page.

Any people depicted in stock imagery provided by Getty Images are models, and such images are being used for illustrative purposes only. Certain stock imagery © Getty Images.

Interior Image Credit: Renee Hanson

This book is printed on acid-free paper.

Contents

Acknowledgements

I would like to thank my son Monzer whom I keep sharing my ideas and perceptions in terms of selecting the title of the book and its' cover. Monzer had a huge impact on this work, without his support this draft-work wouldn't be possible.

I would like to dedicate this work first to my son Monzer in hopes to encourage him in his academic career and inspire him to learn something from it and reap perseverance and success as well to all the members of my family,

Introduction

This book is about an island, a wealthy island. It's a realistic fiction that demonstrates Rose as an evil plan in the Wealthy Island, the island where wealth has been smuggled by unknown smugglers. Smugglers flocked to an island by helicopter plane and smuggled wealth while islanders were busy celebrating their national day.

The author used nonfactual characters in different situations to achieve the task that either occurred in real life or conceivably take place. This book is quite interesting in revealing inappropriate methods of practicing power to control people. Of course, it tells us about the impact of absolute power in a leadership role in the absence of decency, justice, integrity, dignity, freedom, and accountability.

It's an idea of an evil plan that's being implemented by the main character in the book Miss Rose. Her perception is to hack the governing system in the Wealthy Island potentially causes chaos and unnecessary chaos on all islands.

The author encourages readers to study the book and analyze its' narration to the public at large; it's of course, indeed, an unfair intervention in the Wealthy Island from an outsider conspired with the leadership role. It's of course, indeed, an intervention that draws the reader's attention to share it and judge it, in the absence of transparency and collective observations.

Chapter 1

THE FERTILE-ISLAND

A photo of the Fertile Island, June 23, 2001.

On a Fertile-Island, was a beautiful Queen her name was Naya, she was not only queen of the island, she lived on the island. The Island is extraordinarily rich, and Naya was ruling the Island for such a long time. Naya was a good ruler. She was loved by all islanders. She was friendly and popular amongst the islanders of the Island.

The island had large army and all sorts of natural resources. The Island's surrounded by several small Islands, but this Fertile-Island was the best among all in every way, and is much bigger than the other islands in the region.

The population of the Fertile- Island is estimated to be approximately about five million. Half of the population were running business and the rest of the population working in public and private sectors.

The population was increasing rapidly, and that might cause housing problems. The Queen improved the housing condition that is the majority of islanders live and doubles the amount of the housing that is now available to overcome the housing problems.

The natural weather on the island is moderate most of the time. The island is located on low land. The island was full of flowers, trees, fountains, and waterfalls. The location of the Island is extremely attractive, stimulating, and memorizing the eyes.

In spring, islanders enjoy visiting gardens and watching the beauty of nature. Islanders enjoy watching the beauty of the birds' majestic colors as they fly in flocked around waterfalls, while listening to their magical and joyous songs. They enjoyed watching the trickling water spring that runs through the green hilly area mountains. They enjoyed playing hide and seek with kids behind small bushes with joy, and love.

The island is so damp and foggy in the mornings. The sky's always covered with clouds. The sun looks tiny behind the dark clouds in the mornings. The vast majority of Islanders are busy working on farms. They usually work their farms in the mornings and then usually go to their homes in the evenings. They plant and grow all sorts of grains, and their gardens are full of all kinds of fruit as well.

THIS IS THE FERTILE ISLAND

The road's soft, clean, and comfortable for biking and driving vehicles on it. The road had a variety of lights on both sides. The roads are so busy and full of a multitude of cars on weekends; some islanders continued driving on highways to visit their siblings on other islands while some continued driving back at homes.

Islanders do not keep driving old cars on roads, and even the government of the island doesn't allow them to put old cars on roads, the government finances, enforce and help them to have cars in good condition.

Generally, islanders are rich and keep driving new cars on roads to avoid air pollution. They're very seriously keeping their island evergreen all year round, they don't throw trash on the ground at all, and if they do the municipality will charge them.

The young generation on the island would always prefer to ride bikes over vehicles; they love to bike because they want to stay physically fit as well as to protect their urban dwellings from pollution.

The island is well-organized in terms of road service inside and outside downtown. The pedestrians have their sidewalks, bikers have their lanes and even vehicles have their own roads.

The Queen remains continuously encouraged islanders to keep investing in farming sectors. The Queen provided farmers with all farming equipment in need to cultivate their lands. She also visits all farms and talks in person with farmers to make sure that they get everything they needed.

The Queen encourages farmers to utilize large-scale agricultural land to increase crops, during the harvest season; during the harvest, the Queen sends an agriculture committee to all farmers in their fields to buy the production at favourable prices to increase the rate of agricultural production.

The Queen understands the importance of agricultural production; she also understands the importance of green land, and the significance of the encouragement of agricultural production to compete in the international market.

A photo of the Green land, September 20, 2001

The island is remaining rich and green; the grass is remaining rich and green too. The island is covered with green grass in spring and is flourished with enchanting variety of flowers as a rainbow in the blue sky. All among it one can see beautifully busy bees singing and clinging to these outstanding flowers.

YOU CAN NOT SEE THE EARTH, THE GRASS IS RICH AND GREEN THE ISLAND IS REMAINING RICH AND GREEN ALL YEAR ROUND

The Island is surrounded by a high fence that was made of solid bricks. The high fence was built to protect islanders from strangers. A high fence was established to keep the island safe. The island had only one large gate open to the movement of traffic to the world outside.

The Island had well-trained security guards in charge of peace and order in all areas. The security guards work throughout the island all day long. They keep watching all places where islanders gather.

People from other regions would dream to move into and settle down on the island for the following reasons:

- The job wages on the Island are higher in the region and the standard of living is high too.
- There are a lot of different types of job opportunities in public and private sectors.
- There are a lot of youth program and seniors program are made to break isolation.
- There are a lot of different types of festivals to bringing islanders together in downtown.

The Queen of the island had a big palace that was full of gold and silver. The Palace is located in the centre of the island. The palace was considered to be the biggest palace in the region. The palace includes hundred rooms and three big halls for celebrations. The numbers of the working people inside the palace were estimated to be approximately more than three hundred.

LIVING CONDITION IN THE FERTILE-ISLAND

The Queen was very honest and trusted by islanders to keep the Island wealthy. The lifestyle on the island was comfortable, safe, rich, and better in comparison to other Islands in the region.

The social system on the island supports islanders and provided them with aid and food. Islanders receive financial support from the government. All islanders were rich and contented.

The government of the island provides islands with three basics needs:

- Food
- Education
- Medication

Education system in the Fertile-Island

Islanders have had access to all sorts of education. Education is free for all islanders from primary schools to Universities. There were about five hundred schools, hundred colleges in different professional fields and two hundred universities.

GOVERNING SYSTEM

The Queen has had a unique system of governing; one such example, the government institutions have had independently authoritative power.

The rate of crime on the island is almost zero. The dominions of justice and decency in government institutions have played a vital role in reducing the crime rate. There was no corruption or bribes in the government institutions, and even islanders had already rejected the perception of corruption in their all walks of life.

Rose escaped from the military service

One day night, the full moon appeared in the sky, broke darkness and spread light high. The night was quiet. The night wind blows quietly the branches of the trees and shakes them gently. Rose slowly escaped from the Great Island. She slowly walked through woods and jungles for several days and nights. She left the Great Island for the last time.

She escaped from working in the military service. Rose used to work for the Great Island in military service.

After such a long journey, Rose was approaching a fence. The fence was tall and strong. She looked left, and right, up and down all around, there was no security guard. She slowly climbed up the fence and entered the island, in time; it was raining heavily, chilly and windy night, which forced and kept all of the security guards inside their cabin.

It was a good time for the little pretty lady to sneak into the island. It was a good time because the rain forced the security guards to stay in. It was a good time because the chilly wind forced all islanders to stay inside their homes.

The lady carried a small suitcase in her right hand. The suitcase includes some cloth, shoes, necklaces, and rings. Just to name a few. She was in green and on top of that she was wearing a raincoat.

While she was walking toward the palace, she took off the raincoat. The lady looked very magnificent in green while walking towards the palace gate. She has beautiful black hair and eyes.

The security guard was standing at the gate while she was walking toward the palace. The security guard saw her walking, but he did not stop her from entering the palace. He thought wrongly that she is one of the members of the working staff in the palace.

Short description of the Palace:

The palace is noticeably huge. It has many rooms; there were a lot of working ladies in the palace. Ladies work in different jobs. Some ladies work as waitresses for the Queen, some ladies work as waitresses for the guests, some of them work as cooks and some of them work as cleaners. Just to name a few.

The lady went and dressed in white like other waitresses in the palace and started working in the kitchen. She looked very beautiful in her white uniform; she looked very professional in her white uniform, when all waitresses got together in their white uniforms, they look as if they were white snow rose in winter.

Every morning, the Queen sits in the big dining room waiting for special breakfast; the Queen's special breakfast was milk and honey dip donuts. The Queen loves to drink a glass of milk and eat some honey dip donuts in the mornings.

Someday morning, while the Queen was sitting in the dining room waiting for her breakfast, the little beautiful lady in a white uniform brought a glass of milk and some honey dip donuts to the Queen.

The Queen looked at the lady and asked "what is your name."

"My name is Rose." The lady responded.

"Do you know to read and write?" the Queen inquired.

"I am a postgraduate in politics," Rose responded.

"Would you like to come and see me in my office today afternoon?" The Queen requested.

"Yes, I do, gladly" Rose replied.

In the afternoon Rose dressed in blue as the blue sky, and went to the Queen in her office. Rose looked very pretty in blue; the Queen didn't recognize Rose at first.

Rose introduced herself to the Queen. I am the lady whom you met with in the dining room this morning and asked me to come and see you."

The Queen initiates a short social chat with Rose to get to know much more about her previous work experience and academic qualification. The Queen listened attentively while Rose was talking about her personal background.

The Queen eventually congratulated Rose on her successful interview and offered her a high position in the palace. Rose accepted the position and thanked the Queen for the post. Rose was thrilled to meet with the Queen in the palace. As a result, Rose had become the director of the Queen's office.

At the same time, the Queen didn't know Rose works behind closed doors for the interest of the Central Intelligence Bureau (CIB) on Great Island. The Great Island had a plan for the future to smuggle the island's wealth, and in order to get that wealth, the king of the Great Island needed a map and precise information about the island's wealth.

9

In that situation, Rose was going to work for both as a double standard, on one hand, to please the Queen on the island, and on the other, to please the king of the Great Island. Rose had a very difficult task to achieve for the king of the Great Island. Rose is going to get the job done successfully because she had good charisma and opened minded.

Rose prepared her work schedule to manage the two positions at the same time.

The first position is the director of the Queen's office and the second position is to work to for the interest of the king of the Great Island.

Attention!

Rose

Is

Evil

Plan

In

The

Island

Rose promised islanders in many public meetings that she would listen to their claims and work on implementing them.

Practically, she accomplished a lot of positive pilot projects in social services. The whole pilot's projects help shape islanders' lives.

Rose started receiving and reading letters to the Queen. She organizes the Queen's meetings with delegations and visitors. She understood her job well within a short time. Rose played a very vital role in the Queen's office, and then the Queen was thrilled and amazed by Rose's duties in public administration.

Rose managed to settle down on the island and hacked the Queen's governing system successfully. She obtained and studied all confidential government documents in the palace office with the help of other employees. She treated her staff members in the Queen's office with dignity and respect. Everyone liked Rose being in her new job. Rose had become much more famous and well-known in the palace.

Rose had been working on the island for ten years as a director of the Queen's office; she made lots of money and prepared lots of social events in the palace.

She traveled abroad every three months to the Great Island. She traveled to Great Island for fun and feasibly submits reports to the (CIB). The report that Rose submits to the (CIB) includes confidential information about the Fertile Island. Nobody among the security guards in the customs services at the airport would dare to check Rose's luggage while leaving abroad.

One night, the Queen asked Rose to send an invitation letter to all kings and Queens who rule the small islands for dinner parties in the palace. Rose grasped that golden opportunity to build a personal relationship with all Queens who had been attending the dinner party.

All guests went to the dining room to dine, and drink, and then they went to the dance- hall where dance is live till late at night.

At the end of the dinner party, all Queens left the party with a good impression of Rose who organized the event; the Queen also was very pleased with Rose for all the decorations and images that she put in the palace building.

Rose wanted to hack all the other small islands in the region and collects significant information about their locations and properties. Rose luckily met in person with different Queens at different events. Rose convinced different Queens in different events to hire some qualified ladies for their official work.

All Queens agreed and relied on Rose to bring beautiful ladies to different islands. Rose immediately informed the Central Intelligence Bureau (CIB) on the Great Island to provide her with five beautiful ladies from the Great Island.

Rose brought qualified ladies in all small islands. Each lady becomes as a director of the Queen's Office. In doing so, Rose had built a net spy in all small islands.

The net spy designed by Rose on all islands was functioning as an integral part of the CIB on the great Island.

Description of the Great Island

There was also a king of the Great Island. The Great Island is located very far away somewhere from the islands. The name of the king of the Great Island is Ceszor. The Great Island had been developed and improved by its people from all walks of life, in it there were great institutions, and the king was planning in expanding its power to dominate other small islands in the future.

The king built a great industrial revolution. He built factories, schools, colleges, and universities, but however fabric factories on the Great Island were lacking cotton-ore, because of their high demands.

Rose informed the king that small islands had all sorts of raw materials that he was looking for. The king needed to know in detail about the capacity of power and natural resources in those islands. To achieve that task; the king sent Rose as a spy on the island to collect data and send it to the intelligence spy on the Great Island.

Rose told the Queen of the island to open business and trade with the king of the Great Island, but the Queen was not interested in opening international trade with the Great Island, owing to several considerations, one of those considerations, was to stay away from the free-trade,

The other consideration is that the Fertile-Island had already established a unique trade business system with all small islands to exchange all types of products. In other words, the Queen was very satisfied and contented in every way.

Chapter 2

THE HARBOUR

Hanson, R. (2022). *The Queen Mary arrives in the Harbor.* Kitchener city, ON, Canada

THE HARBOUR OF THE Fertile- Island received the ship (the Queen Mary). The Queen Mary was a big commercial ship belongs to the Great Island. The ship is famous for trade and well-known. The ship started its journey from the Great

Island in winter and returns home in summer. It traveled all around the world. It went up to Cape Town in South Africa.

The ship sometimes returns to the Great Island late owing to the bad weather. The weather sometimes gets worse and worse. When the weather gets bad, the captain of the ship would sail to the nearest shore. The ship stays at the shore until the weather gets better.

Sometimes The ship runs out of food and water, and the staff would need to have enough food and drinking water, in that condition, the captain would also look for the nearest port to stay for a while and leave.

Some day early in the morning, the harbour of the Fertile Island received the Queen Mary; the marine security saw the ship from a mile away that it was coming to the harbour. While the ship was approaching, the captain of the ship told the marine security that he was coming to the seashore to get some food and drinking water.

He had been sailing on the sea for twenty days. He added that "on board some men and women had become sick due to the bad food and water."

The captain requested the marine security to allow him to admit his patients to the hospital for medical treatment. The marine security was very supportive, but they do not have power to allow the captain to admit them.

The head of the marine security in communication with the Queen's head office about the ship "the Queen Mary" in detail. The Queen administered the marine security to allow the Queen Mary to stay at the harbour and provide it with all necessary measures; she also instructed the marine security to allow the captain of the ship and his crew to enter the island.

In reality, the five beautiful ladies were not sick, but they were only pretending that they were sick. They played that role to mislead the marine security to let them in.

The men were truly sick and they had been admitted to different hospitals to receive their medical care, and they stayed in the hospital for several days.

A week later, they recovered from their illness. They went to the palace and met with the director of the Queen's office Miss Rose. They introduced themselves as businessmen looking for an opportunity to invest in the island.

Rose attempted to help them to run business in the island, she introduced the businessmen to the Queen but the Queen disapproved and opposed the idea. Rose conveyed the Queen's refusal message to the businessmen; they requested Rose to convince the Queen to let them run business, eventually they get permission with chance of investment in all islands.

Rose had trained those five ladies with a crash course related to security affairs. She also provided them with special code information to communicate confidentially with each other. They were also being trained to use information technology to hack the governing system in all small islands.

After three days, Rose met with the captain of the ship in the Queen hotel on the seashore. The captain handed the Queen a confidential letter from the king of the Great Island. Rose took the letter and looked at it in her office. She found the letter full of instructions and protections; the letter was talking about the reality of the island's wealth.

, the islanders were astonished to see such businessmen on business in the city hall. Vast islanders don't welcome foreigners from the Great Island, because they read a lot about the king of the Great Island, they learned he was so hypocritical and a dictator.

Islanders respect the leadership role that listens, assists, and supports islanders, they do respect the leaders who believe in human rights, equality, dignity, and decency.

Islanders were intellectual to comprehend what the king policy of the Great Island looks like, they refused to welcome the king in their region, the Queen also rejected the concept of building a good relationship with the Great Island, because she knows the king potentiality.

In reality, all those men and women on the ship were working for CIB interest, they came to know the exact amount of the natural resources in all islands, and then they could be able to send reports to the king.

The five ladies have already formed their plan into five committees, each committee is composed of five persons, and each committee represents a country and its language. Each committee is sent to a different small island to run a business.

Within a few months later, the businessmen opened schools of languages on different islands. In other words, one island had a school for the French language, and the other island had a school for the English language, just to name a few.

Schools turned into busy Centres with people who love learning French to go to France, and some schools become busy with people who like learning English to go to the Great Island.

Those foreign schools for foreign languages on all islands allowed people from different parts of the world to come. They visit the island to identify islanders' heritage. The small islands started opening up for all kinds of foreigners to watch, work at institutions and run successful businesses.

The Queen of the island had a younger brother, his name is David. He had been to Great Island for educational studies at the University of Oxford. He had been living there for five years. He attained a Bachelor of Arts in political science.

David speaks two languages, English and French. Based on his academic qualifications, the Queen nominated him as the Minister of foreign affairs. David took over the position and started working in the field of education and transportation. During his first tenure in the position; he signed several agreements with Australia to develop transportation and education.

Some studies show that Australia had built a great relationship with all islands and also signed several agreements on business, such as education, and information technology. Australia understands that the Fertile-Island is the right country for investment and stability for all people in different parts of the world.

David had been working on different projects that help shape the beauty of the island. During his tenure, the island had become well-connected with all small islands by highways, go trains, and Airplanes.

During his tenure, David admitted that Rose also did great accomplishments in the Fertile-Island. For instance, she opened hundred community services and welfare system for all islanders to live in peace.

Someday evening, While David was in a meeting with Rose; his eyes fell on documents on Rose's table entitled: "*confidential information about the wealthy island*." David wanted to grab the documents and look at them, but Rose quickly removed them from the table.

David frowned and left the meeting. Rose instantly informed the Queen about the event, but later on, the Queen intervened and settled down the dispute. The Queen didn't know Rose was working for the C.I.B.

David went to his office and started thinking of the documents on Rose's table. He asked himself the following questions related to the documents on Rose's table.

- Why did Rose hide the documents?
- Why did Rose refuse to let me look at documents?
- Which type of confidential information was included in those documents?

All the above questions that have been raised by David required clear-cut answers. He invited some employees working at Rose office to find out the resource of those documents, but all the employees whom he inquired had no idea for those documents.

David met with his sister Queen Naya and told her in detail about what he saw and what happened during the meeting, the Queen did not show much interest in investigating such an event, because she put great confidence in Rose. The Queen simply responded to David, please don't worry about Rose and do not push further behind something that we were not quite sure about it.

David respected his sister Naya very much and he did not want to make her uncomfortable, he was quite sure that there was something going on behind closed doors with Rose, but he didn't find out what motivated Rose to keep those confidential documents away from him. He was very curious, to know.

David understood that the Queen ignored what he had been talking about from the very beginning. However, David is very smart and knew that the Great Island had a plan to expand and take over all small islands. He knew that from some articles that he had already read in the library at the University of Oxford.

David usually used his critical thinking while reading or listening to the news, he was very intelligent in analyzing and criticizing issues, he never accepts things without using his critical thinking.

David was a young guy in his family. He wanted to get married to the royal family in one of the other islands. The Queen was very pleased to support him in getting married from the other islands. David's father had passed away ten years ago, he lived with his mother. His mother's name was Asia.

In June 1900, the preparation of the wedding party took place in the queen's palace. The whole island streets were decorated with different colors, green, red, yellow, and white lights. The decoration of the various lights on the island at night made its night its day made.

The city hall was becoming extremely overcrowded with islanders from different islands attending the wedding party. The best orchestra and singers had come to sing at the wedding, and the best dancers had come to dance at the wedding as well.

The wedding party had been continuing for a week in the city hall, companies by gigantic free meals and drinks.

There was also a lot of precious gold and silver that had been distributed to the audience and singers by the Queen's staff. Some islanders had been given some big envelopes including some money orders to be cashed at the National bank.

The island is very rich and content with gold and silver. The Queen came to the wedding party along with Queens and the kings of the other islands. It was very beautiful weather at that time, it was spring and the full moon appeared in the sky. The sky was clear from the clouds; the rise of the full moon reduced the appearance of the bright stars in the sky.

The wedding party had ended the late night, and the bride and the bridegroom both left the wedding for their honeymoon in one of the best hotels on an island near the shore. The hotel's name was the Queen hotel. It was located near the seashore.

Someday evening, the weather was good and the wind blows very fresh and alert. David told his wife Sandra that the weather is moderate near the seashore, so let us go for a walk and come back to the hotel. They were still in their honeymoon days. They both went out for a walk by the side of the seashore.

While they were walking together, they were looking at the waves rolling behind waves. It was evening time, and the sun wasn't very hot. While they were walking and talking to one another, a gang of people approached them while they were patrolling. David and his wife had been shot dead at short range by a gang and ran away.

It was shocking news to the Queen and all islanders. The security failed to identify the killers and the whole news began talking about the event. The investigation committee continued for several days, eventually, the investigation committee found out that the killer who had committed the crime had already fled the island by the steamer to an unknown country.

After the successful assassination attempt of the foreign minister Mr. David, Rose had become the director of the queen's office and the foreign minister. Rose had become very close to the Queen.

Rose devoted much time meeting with islanders on the downtown road to learn from them about the news of others. That sort of social meeting with ordinary islanders' downtown had also made Rose well-known and respected amongst islanders at large.

Islanders had been talking about the death of the minister of foreign affairs for a while in shops, stores, and markets. They were not accustomed to hearing about failing or successful assassination attempts on the island.

They raised several questions and wait for answers. One such example:

What will happen to islanders in the future if the government fails to catch the criminals and bring them to justice?

Rose promised islanders to take all necessary measures to find out the criminals and bring them to justice. She knows that the C.I.B was behind the crime of killing the foreign minister.

At the same time, the organizations of human rights (O.H.R) on the island are getting involved. The head office of the (O.H.R) had stated that it would soon question Miss Rose about The assassination of the former foreign minister, and a spokesperson declared the (O.H.R) working group could launch an investigation on murder crime once Queen Rose has been responded. But that probably not be enough, because now the assassination of the former foreign minister has become a question of face for Rose. She knows what all the other rulers and islanders of small islands are saying about her.

They're saying "why did Miss Rose let this assassination of the former foreign minister take place?"

At the same time, the international humanitarian organization had also sent a very strong message to both Miss Rose and the nation that this murder crime is very serious and requires serious investigation with the presence of a committee composed of members from all human rights organizations.

Chapter 3

NAYA'S FAMILY IN ISLAND

A photo of the Wide road, June 23, 2001

NAYA'S GRANDFATHER, LEER, WAS THE KING OF THE ISLAND.

Leer ruled the island for twenty years, he was a good ruler. He loved reading political books. He devoted much of his time reading political books. He always wakes up early in the morning and reads. He also does physical exercises every morning. He learned a lot about politics. He was reading and understanding the value of becoming a good ruler.

He put much of what he had been learning from the political books into practice. He also had a good charisma; his charisma assisted him to be respected amongst islanders. He supported all islanders and demonstrated justice at the highest levels of the Island.

Leer had become sick in the last days of his ruling tenure on the island. He got a severe fever for a month lying on a bed. He used to do a lot of physical activities and eat healthy food. The severe fever prevented him from doing gymnastics.

He didn't have a previous chronic disease, but from time to time he was complaining about severe fever. He had multiple blood work and when the result came out there was nothing serious.

Leer had been in hospital for a month before he passed away. The doctor discovered that the severe fever was caused by malaria, king Leer was seventy-five years old when he was becoming sick.

Doctors in the hospital did all the necessary efforts to save his life, but all of their attempts were unsuccessful. He died at the age of seventy-five.

Islanders were wondering who was going to be the successor, the king knew that he was going to die, but he did not nominate his successor. He left that vacant rank for islanders to decide.

Islanders elected his wife Lisa to be the Queen of the island. Lisa is very well educated, she also learned a lot from the king during his tenure in power; however that doesn't mean she prepared herself for the leadership. She was learning about politics from the king because he was sharing with her several decision-making.

What did she learn from the previous king?

She believes in open discussion, and consultation with others for decision-making, for that reason, she formed a large cabinet of ministries to work together and decide together for any decision-making.

The Islanders elected Lisa to be the Queen of the island. They thought positively that she was going to be nice and kind to them in every way.

Lisa had become the Queen of the island. She did some Cabinet reshuffles in all ministries on the island to make sure that the system of the Government functions to meet the requirements of the islanders' will.

In fact, the Queen learned a lot of skills from the previous king Leer. The king who used to read about politics was a good ruler. When Lisa took over, she already learned the wisdom from her husband while he was in power; she would put what she had been learning from the previous king into practice.

Islanders liked Lisa to be in power because she did not deprive them of their benefits. She made them much richer than ever before. She supports them to run businesses on the island. She forgives them for paying taxes to the government.

The majority of islanders run small businesses in town, which is a type of small-scale industry that creates lots of job opportunities for local and international students on summer vacation.

Also, islanders have opportunities to take out government loans with low-interest rates to expand their business in town they will. Additionally, the government encourages them to import goods from the international market.

The government believes in perfect competition in all sorts of products on the island, which kind of open market helps make consumers to have options of products in the market, and at the same time the price of all products will remain sustainable.

Lisa studied in France and learned to speak French fluently. During her tenure, she built a strong business relationship between France and small islands. In time, France was not in a position to invade or lead some conspiracies against other countries.

In time, France was looking for a good partner to do business in different fields. The king of France was considered to be one of the best rulers in Europe. He loved to keep peace and stability in the region.

In that situation, the Queen allowed such a good country "France" to share business for the mutual benefits. The Queen knows that the king wanted to run business and develop his land; she signed with him several agreements on business and trade.

The trade between the two countries was doing well and nothing negative happened to break the relationship between them for years and years.

The island had a great army; it was not easy for an outsider to hack the governing system of the island. The governing system was well-protected by IT from hackers. The Queen had IT experts work day and night to keep the government system secure.

The Queen had a strong character, intelligence, and was kind in every way. She built a lot of recreation places for islanders who like to spend some time with their families. The majority of Islanders would love to be with their families on weekends.

The Queen had been ruling the island for ten years. She had a beautiful daughter her name is Asia. Asia had pretty golden hair and beautiful captivating eyes. Asia studied on the island and graduated from the University of Island in social studies. She loved supporting islanders with everything they need.

The Queen taught her daughter at an earlier age how to read and write. Asia had been reading new travel books to several interesting places in the world. She loved reading travel books. When she grew up, she will be remembering those lovely places in her mind. She will travel abroad to see the sights and learn about other nations. She got the conception of traveling from reading new travel books, which told her exciting stories about other countries and that made her intention to travel when she grew up.

Now the time has come for Asia to put those images of reading travel books into practice. She started visiting all small islands and other places in real life around the world. While she was traveling abroad, she got an opportunity to interact with other people. During her visitation she learnt much. She got an opportunity to make new friends, and understands the value of friendship.

The Queen was kind to Asia and let her do whatever she likes. During visitations, Asia perceived many poor places. She noticed some places require some kind of help, and she wanted to help some of them.

Asia built a lot of social communities on the island. She also built many medical centers and community developments in poor countries. She supplied all medical centers with medical aids and financial assistance to keep them vibrant.

Every Friday evening, Asia goes down- Street downtown and meets with islanders. She shares different ideas with them. She socializes with one another. She gets to understand their requirements.

Once upon a time, Lisa received an invitation from Norway to participate in a seminar entitled *"Abuse of human rights."* She talked about the respect for human rights on the island. She proved that the island fully respects human rights, the island is considered to be among one of the best five countries in the world that fully respects human rights in terms of the freedom of speech, movement, and freedom of expression.

At the end of the seminars, all members agreed with Lisa that the island is considered to be a unique model in terms of women's rights and freedom of expression.

The seminar put several proposals on the discussion table to be negotiated in the next meeting. One such example,

- How do we help to protect women's rights in some places where the abuse of women is still alive and kicking?
- How do we contribute to improving women's rights?
- How do we contribute to stopping abusing women's rights?
- How do we contribute to stopping abusing power in violating human rights?

The members of the seminar asked Lisa to come up with some new ideas pertaining women's rights, all members believe that Lisa would come up with great opinions in the next seminar. In time, the leader of the Seminars promised all participants will be given an equal right to talk in the seminar.

Lisa promised the members of the seminar she would come up with effective perspectives that might help shape women situation. She added that "the abuse of women's right is still alive and kicking, as a result a lot of women are suffering from injustice and oppression.

Lisa returned to the island and immediately held a meeting with the cabinet ministers. She informed them that the right time has come to resign. She added "It is time to open up the governing system for islanders to rule the island. It is time for the system of the royal family to step down for others to share power."

Islanders rejected the idea of the new change. But the Queen had already resigned and called for an elected democratically government from all islanders. She insisted on her resignation. She convinced islanders that were the time for a change.

Islanders had no other choice to request rather than Asia. Asia runs for the presidential election and eventually, she won the election. Asia had become the first Queen elect on the island.

In time, the whole world's news was talking about the transitional power on the island. All islanders were pleased with the new Queen elect.

Asia immediately held a public meeting in front of the palace and claimed islanders to form an opposition party that could help shape the Government's performance and accountability in every way.

Asia deliberately studied the situation on the island. She intended to make islanders live in wealth, peace, and happiness, she formed several associations on the island, for instance,

- An agricultural association which was required to follow up community services in charge of watering gardens in the city.
- The traffic unit was responsible for assisting islanders to understand safe and responsible driving, to train islanders to have access to all kinds of support that they needed. In doing so, islanders had become much more confident in driving and traffic laws that could help traffic move safely in downtown.

In addition, the traffic move in the city looks in good shape, and the implementation of the traffic laws reduced frequent accidents on roads, in the meantime, islanders accustomed to follow the traffic laws and drive safely in the city to avoid accidents.

One important thing on the island was that the government enforced tough traffic laws for drivers who go over speed limit in town, a driver may easily lose his driving license if he does not respect the traffic laws, regardless of his position or ethnicity. "No one above the laws"

The mother of the Queen elect had resigned and refused to have a private security. She wanted to live a normal and simple life in a small townhouse with her little dog. She wanted to interact with islanders and share stories. She opens a big nightclub for women to join and have a social chat.

Lisa visits the nightclub every night. She likes staying late night at the club. She was about seventy years old at that time, but she looks as if she was forty. She was looking very young. She loved riding a bike and visiting communities on the island.

She sometimes thought about how she could help poor islanders. Someday, she went to look for poor islanders on the island to help, she spent all day biking up and down the city, but she did not find any poor islanders to support.

She went to her daughter's office and found her in a meeting with some high-level delegation who had just arrived from France. The Queen invited her and introduced her to a meeting, "this is my mother, and she was the Queen of the island." In time, Lisa asked her mother if she would need help. But the mother said that "I have just come to let you know that I have been biking up and down the city all day long to find some poor islanders to assist, but I could find none I could see none.

The delegation was shocked to hear that good news. One of the members of the delegation spoke out "we came from a rich country, but still do have so many beggars in the streets. Most of them may die of cold in the winter because they did not have shelters to go."

The older brother of Naya was the general commander of the army. His name is Ferdinand. Ferdinand was working very closely with other commanders in the army. He developed and improved the benefits for all soldiers in the army. He divided the big army into three units,

- The Navy unit,
- The Police unit,
- The Air Force unit.

The three units of the army have been working collaboratively, each unit of the army is being responsible for a different piece of work, and they all combine to maintain stability, peace and keep order on island.

- The police unit is in charge of keeping order on the island. Organize traffic transportation, helps islanders in the city to be safe and secure at all times.

- The Navy unit protects the harbour and the island from anomie's plan to occupy the island under any circumstances. The Navy unit was well trained in duties and ready to react at all levels.
- The air force unit is stronger and also well-advanced in training and in monitoring information and investigation. The air force unit is small but it was considered to be one of the most advanced and strongest air forces in all regions.

Most of the employees in the air force graduated from the Royal Military College on the island. Those who did not graduate from college had also been training in the High-tech college school for two years to fly an Air defense plane in times of war.

Ferdinand on weekends disguises himself and goes out on the streets of the island to meet with islanders in shops, and malls. He would like to see the condition of islanders on the ground and compare it with the daily working report.

Ferdinand would be able to obtain direct information from islanders whom he met in public and private places. He works hard to get benefit from all information that he collected through his weekly tour around the island. That was what made Ferdinand popular amongst islanders who pin their hopes on him, and indeed he succeeded in fulfilling their promises.

On Friday morning, Ferdinand was in a small car driving to the military area. While he was waiting at the intersection for the signal to change from red to green, an old man was running by the side of the road stepped on a piece of rock and fell down. Ferdinand instantly stepped out the car and rushed to pick him up from the ground.

He called the emergency service (911) to help save the old man's life, he was injured on his head, and his head was bleeding. Ferdinand had been waiting for half an hour to meet with the first aid services to help them get the right information and then after that, he left for his work.

There were so many good stories about the commander Ferdinand in terms of supporting ordinary people on the island.

Someday morning, Ferdinand read an article in the newspaper articulating that the Community Centre in the south of the island will be going on a cleaning campaign. The cleaning campaign will be working on the new extension street twenty-five on Saturday in the morning. He immediately rang up them and confirmed that he would be more than happy to join the cleaning campaign on Saturday morning.

On Saturday morning Ferdinand joined the campaign and worked with them on cleaning the area, most of the volunteers were university students. He has been working with them for several hours. Nobody identified the commander of the army was with them in the cleaning campaign.

The next day, they learned from the news that the commander of the army was participating in the cleaning campaign as a volunteer to help keep the area clean.

Ferdinand traveled on vacations to other districts in the region to support people who are in need of help; he also built several medical Centers for villagers who live in the countryside.

Some evidence proved that Ferdinand used to spend half of his salary on poor people who live in different parts of the world. He designed a pilot project to combat poverty in poor areas.

He also opened two big schools in the countryside, one school for boys and the other one for girls.

Ferdinand has become well-known in the countryside and small villages, he was hoping to see all youth live happily and contented in this worldly life.

Ferdinand stated the following stanza about life:

Life means joy if you enjoy
Life means fun if you dump
Life means peace if you believe
Life means give if you take
Life means smile if you frown
Life means love if you hate
Life means share if you care

Chapter 4

WORKING WOMEN

The working women's history in the Fertile Island referred to centuries of years. The beginning of the development of working women was depending on families' activities on farms, homes, offices, and communities at large.

On farms, each family member of men and women were working together hand in hand to grow vegetables and other food products. That was the beginning of the working women in communities.

The working women with men were not planning, but it was happening naturally and traditionally that women could work on farms to help the family to bring food to the table.

Later on, the island developed tremendously and improved in all public and private sectors, as this great development has been taking place, there were more job opportunities than ever before.

Most working women believe that the freedom to go to work is the first step toward women's contribution to the community. In the meantime, women have been learning and serving the community in all fields.

We observed several ideas from working women in the private and public sectors. One such example, Sandra shares her perception in the following discussion. "Working means to me," Sandra said. A government employee, "is much more not getting money, but through my work, I would definitely feel that my "existence" that I have a value that I could be in a position to contribute to the community in the place where I live,"

Some working women believe that we're facing various practical and other problems in the workplaces; one of the main problems is accommodations, sometimes the head of the family refused to let his wife move to another place and live by herself.

That type of problem had been taking place on the island at the beginning of the government services, but lately the employee, either he or she could be able to move with his family to the new place where the government offered him all the requirements.

A single woman at the workplace was allowed to stay with their family or relatives, but that situation was few women enjoy it because a single woman who lives with her relative should respect the family rules in terms of going out and home duties.

"I do not want to live with my relatives, I work in the bank that means at the end of the day spending my leisure time with my relatives while chatting with my friends online, with my relatives I may have nothing in common to talk about," Anne said.

Few young women believe that living with other families means that they were not free in their social life. For many young single girls, the housing problem is so acute that they are forced to go back to their homes on the islands and surrender their hopes of a career, or further educational studies.

Some other women believe that marriage is as good as a means of allowing them much more freedom of movement to interact and mix socially with others.

The good news, in marriage, women nowadays have had the right to select. This means not only the freedom to select whom they wanted to marry, rather than earlier in old day's history of the island that their husbands selected for them by their family.

All old traditions and customs that led to marriage and social life have been changed for the better, and the government of the island set a law that protects all civil rights.

"In old days, marriage for some girls was not welcoming, that they preferred to stay single, they against it unless there is a real change in the attitude of some elders towards women in the way they treat them."

Louis said.

Ten years ago, Most women devoted much of their time at home working in the kitchen or walking around gossiping, they believed that it was really difficult for them to work and raise kids at the same time, but nowadays, life has changed and it is possible for women to work and raise kids at the same time.

For most women on the island, the freedom to go to the workplace was happening a long time ago. They have their own responsibilities for their lives themselves and make absolutely free decisions in all walks of life.

Recently the lifestyle of all families on the island had completely changed for much better than ever, one such example, more than seventy percent of the government employees in the high position were women.

Women took a vital role in all public and private sectors, most directors and managers in private sectors were women, and most of the high positions in the government were women too.

Women proved their ability and productivity in all different departments, that does not mean men were not working in high positions, but the majority of high positions were filled with women because they were dedicated, devoted, motivated, compassionate, and honest.

Each country would improve by its people and that would have been seen in the Fertile Island that had developed rapidly by its islanders both men and women.

There were equal wages for islanders both men and women in the lovely land.

The island was considered the first country in the world that gave women their full rights to be equal with men in all positions in terms of wages and promotions. The men on the island respect women very much and support women very much because the study on the island proved that women were honest in terms of complying with laws and orders.

The study on the island also showed that the percentage of women graduating from colleges and universities was greater and higher than men. That means there was no illiteracy on the island.

Everyone either man or woman knows his/her rights and responsibilities towards the island and their families.

Some neighbouring countries sent their people to the island for workshop training at some professional colleges to learn some new skills and qualities to apply when they return to their homes.

The island profoundly accepts international students to study at universities and provided them with free medical treatment and accommodations, some international students received some financial assistance from the island for their cost of living too.

Annually the ministry of education offered international students from other countries one hundred scholarships in different fields of education, that kind of support also drew the attention of the nation to acknowledge that the island is one of the best five countries in the world for people to live a decent life. So many students graduated in science, and education and work in international organizations.

Most of the islanders do not have financial problems, because the government supported them, however, they still needed to work for the government to contribute to the development of the sectors.

The rate of unemployment is zero on the island, there were a lot of job opportunities for both men and women, and many sectors reserve posts for fresh graduate students to gain work experience and financial assistance.

Those job opportunities were opening for both domestic and international students. Some international students apply for citizenship to live on the island for the rest of their life, some do not.

The government of the island permits international students to work on the island after their graduation if they are interested, the government did not force them to do so, and students would do that by their own choice and willingness.

The government invests in its people to study which is why the island was developing rapidly and successfully, and everyone was pleased with what he had and what he achieved and received from the government.

To, believe it or not, the government did not have prisoners, thieves or criminals to be sent to jail, yes, indeed, the government had established a prison for prisoners, but the prison was remaining empty because there were no crimes in the island.

The police only managed to be in charge of keeping peace and order on the island. The police were very educated and firm in applying rules and kind at the same time to islanders on roads, shops, markets, and homes.

Most of the police inspectors were women, who graduated from universities and worked in police offices to help shaped peace and order on the island. They were very smart and honest in implementing regulations without discrimination.

The campaign to offer education to the islanders had already been reflected in the whole working place over the past thirty years. A great achievement, but that had led to new job opportunities. There were enough teachers and enough funds from the government for all essential learning materials, particularly curricula. As long as education is one of the fundamental rights for islanders, most women would get a chance to learn and work.

The government of the island had also focused on technical education as the most important for development, yes, indeed, the educational skills most essential to the improvement of our island are technical, agricultural, managerial, and health science.

Here is the list of Universities on the Fertile Island that offers full-time studies.

Guide ——Fall/summer programs, courses-continue your education with the full-time studies- all the following institutions designed to students upgrade their skills and enhance their career.

Continuing Education/programs & courses are available on the following institutions:

- Queen's University
- Island University
- International University

- Medical College for Science Studies
- International University College for public Administration
- Business College/Hotel Management College
- Open University/Lisa College/ David College/Queen College.

The variety of delivers and support are available with all universities and colleges full-time and part-time studies made it the right choice for many students to learn professional development.

Are you an internationally educated student looking to work in the island?

Apply now to a new tuition –free program!

Study at any University on the island, including Queen College, as a part of the island's plan to enhance the student's workforce.

Registration is now available for students who look for additional education to work on the island.

Do you know you can achieve an island Queen College credential full-time, in person?

Study the Queen College Certificate, Diploma, advanced diploma, degree or graduate certificate you would like to achieve with the convenience of studying full-time, in person.

The Queen College is also committed to offering flexible studying options –part-time studying diplomas and certifications in different professional learning programs.

To get started now Please visit the Universities and Colleges programs for available programs:

Island-Universities-Colleges.ca.edu/programs.

Chapter 5

AN ORPHAN GIRL

Rebecca was a little orphan girl. She could not remember how old would she have been at that time, maybe nine or ten years old. She lives with her brother John in the countryside. She goes to school in the mornings and returns home in the evenings; she was in grade eight. She was very smart at school. She was very friendly with her classmates. She likes to help and socialize with others. She likes learning much about social studies in class.

The school Staff is very pleased with Rebecca because she always behaves well. She was one of the best students in the class and much more popular in the school.

John was working in the mines. He lives with his wife Lucie. They have no children. John spends thirty days working in the mines. He gets paid very little per month. He gets paid $20 per month.

John lives with his father. After the death of his father, he owned the house. He does not have to worry about paying rent. What he had earned from the mines helped him to bring food to the table.

Rebecca was living with Lucie while John working in the mines. Lucie treated Rebecca unkindly in the absence of John. Lucie made Rebecca do all sorts of home dishes. Additionally, Rebecca was watering the garden every morning.

During John's presence, Lucie treats Rebecca nicely. In reality, Rebecca was not pleased with Lucie. Even though, she did not tell John that she was unhappy here at home. She did not want to make problems in the house unnecessarily. In time, Rebecca lives under pressure. That pressure made her remember the kindness of her parents.

The pressure made Rebecca plan to visit the graveyard. In the marches where there were parents and three elder brothers buried.

It was winter, cold, and windy in the morning; there were a lot of mists and foggy in the sky. It was so difficult to walk in the morning outdoors. Rebecca preferred to go out in the afternoon. In the afternoon, there were few clouds cover the sun and that make the sun gives a gentle slap on the face.

Rebecca determined to visit the graveyard every Saturday afternoon. She picks some flowers from the garden that she was watering to place them on the graves. She usually spends a minimum of two hours sitting by the side of the graves and grieving.

On Saturday week, many people visit their siblings buried in the graveyard. Someday evening, one rich family from the Fertile-Island visits the graveyard. They come in a group to walk around and see if the graveyards require some preparations.

Rebecca often returns home at the sunset from the graveyard. Lucie does not care about Rebecca if she goes out or comes into late at night.

Someday evening while John was sitting in the backyard of the house, he perceived Rebecca was not home. He asked his wife about Rebecca, "I did not know where she goes". His wife Lucie answered.

John gets mad at Lucie; because she did not know where Rebecca goes. While they were quarrelling with one another, Rebecca arrived home with a big envelope in her hands.

"Where have you been? Johan asked.

"I have been to my parents," Rebecca said.

What did you say? John inquired.

"I was with my parents in the graveyard" Rebccca responded.

John began weeping and tears dropped from his eyes, he added, "you did an excellent job. John stood up and kissed Rebecca while tears run down his cheeks."

"Are you living happily with us? John investigated.

"You and I are not happy as long as we missed our parents in the early stage of our lives" Rebecca responded.

While they were talking about their parents, Lucie came to the backyard with a cattle of tea in her hands. John took it and placed it on the tea table. John kept asking Rebecca to tell him about the big envelope that he had seen in her hands.

Rebecca told him that "it could be a surprise, let us have tea together first and then we could talk about it." After a few minutes, she told him that "the envelope was going to be a nice story and it was going to be the beginning of our life journey.

"Last week, I met with one lady in the graveyard. She was also coming to visit. While she was walking up and down the graveyards, she saw me sitting beside my parent's graves." Rebecca said. He added, "The lady approached and looked at me while I was sitting beside my parents. I saw her taking out a pen and a piece of paper from her suitcase and writing down my parents' names. And then she turned at me and asked the following questions:

"Do you visit your parents every week?"

"Yes I do visit my parents every week," I said.

What is your name?

"My name is Rebecca."

"It is very kind of you to visit your parents every week" the lady commented.

"I love them, I miss them keep remembering them in my heart" Rebecca commented too.

She added "The lady left me in that difficult situation, it was a very emotional moment, I could see tears running down her cheeks while talking to me. She simply walked away without saying goodbye.

All that discussion occurred last week in the graveyard, so this Saturday weekend, I went back to the graveyard and found this big envelope being placed beside my father's name, and on top of the envelope it was my name written in upper case letter REBECCA. I still did not know who write it and what was in it?" Rebecca explained.

Let us open it now and read it out together. I am glad my brother to see what the future brings to us now. Rebecca said.

Rebecca and John opened the envelope and they found in it a written letter, a money order with a hundred dollars, an open ticket to the Fertile Island by the steamer the Queen Mary.

John started reading the letter loud while Rebecca and Lucie were listening attentively.

Dear daughter Rebecca,

House No 25
The countryside, the village,
25/8/53

My name is Lisa, I used to be the Queen of the fertile Island, now I am retired but I am still active doing some other social activities in the communities at large.

I have had the experience of talking with a lady here on the Fertile Island, the lady whom you met in the graveyard; she is one of our working people in the mission. The lady told us about your difficult situation and how much you were suffering. She told us that you have had missed your parents when you were a little girl;

You did remember your parents, your parents are always in your heart, your parents are alive in your eyes, you keep remembering them, and you keep visiting them in the graveyard every Saturday, that gives you peace and comfort.

> *We decided now is the time for action to*
> *reward you as a great woman in our mission by*
> *inviting you to be one of our islanders, therefore,*
> *we requested you to come quickly to the Fertile*
> *Island. Come to the city hall, Fertile-Island,*
> *and there we will be giving you some advice,*
> *we will be giving you free accommodation, and*
> *free bus transportation, where the expenditure*
> *will not be important.*

> *Many greetings*
> *Lisa, previous Queen of the Island*

Rebecca was very pleased because the idea of leaving the marches came from the great royal family on the Fertile Island. She was very thrilled, because her dreams come true, but in time, she was unhappy to leave John and his wife in poverty.

John was very excited to hear that his sister would be in a good place where her life would change for the better and forever. In time, John would miss Rebecca, because he loves her and she loves him. John added, "Good luck, and when you have had time please remember us, and when you have had time please talk to us, and when you have had time please visit us, and even if you could support us that would be kind of you."

"You know, john works hard in the mines to bring food to the table, and also I work hard to take care of dishes, life here in the countryside is not easy, but we are used to it and love it," Lucie said.

John already told his friends that Rebecca will be leaving soon for the Fertile-Island. He invited all of his friends for a dinner party. It was spring, and people can have time to spend together in the back yard of John's house and they can have dinner and party at the same time.

People have come to dinner party with some gifts for Rebecca while leaving for the Fertile Island. Rebecca thanked all of them for the gifts and promised them to revisit the village someday.

John lives so far from the river where the Queen Mary sails to the Fertile Island, the place where john lives had no cars. He rented a horse carriage from his neighbour to drop his sister to the seashore to catch the Queen Mary.

All villagers have come to say farewell to Rebecca and offered her good wishes. John put Rebecca's luggage in the carriage, while Rebecca was standing gazing at the villagers. Rebecca's tears were streaming down her cheeks. In the meantime, Lucie cried out loud when the horse carriage jerked.

The horse carriage left for the seashore, it took four hours to get there, and John was with his sister in the horse carriage. Rebecca did not tell him that she has a hard time living with Lucie.

Rebecca told John to be always nice to his wife and other villagers. She promised him to revisit the marches and the graveyard; she told him as soon as she settled down she would work to bring John and Lucie to the wealthy island. She added, "She will never forget John's support and the lovely days that she had been living together in the countryside. However, she would do whatever she can to get them out of poverty."

John and Rebecca spent four hours on the horse carriage until they reached the sea shore. The sailor welcomed them with a broad smile and provided them with food and water. He informed them that the Queen Mary is coming to the seashore shortly. You should not have to worry now, because you arrived on time. The sailor asked them to wait for a while and the Queen Mary will appear soon.

"The only passenger who was leaving now is my sister Rebecca, and here is the ticket," John told.

"The sailor collected the ticket and answered that is fine.

"I reserved a comfortable seat for you and a bed to sleep in if you would like. Your ticket is first-class; you have all facilities, food, drink, and books to read if you will. The journey to the Fertile Island would take fifteen days." The sailor confirmed.

"Thank you so much for letting me knows," Rebecca commented.

The sailor also went further and informed in detailed information. "The Queen Mary was going all around the world. It started from the Great Island and went over the Atlantic Ocean and crossed Cape Town and returned here. The whole journey usually takes three months to reach the cape-town and three months to return to the Great Island.

The Queen Mary is the best among all ships in terms of services and time management. It is a very strong ship and above all, much more popular among passengers. I saw sometimes some passengers have had to wait for a while to book because of the high seasons." He added that, look over there; the Queen Mary has just arrived. Please follow me to the boarding checkpoint. Now you could say goodbye to your brother and follow me to get into the steamer. Excuse me, sir it is not allowed to accompany your sister from this checkpoint, for security reasons. Do not worry about your luggage now; we have a reporter who will take care of it. You will receive your luggage when you get there on the wealthy island.

Please leave it here and our reporter will take it into the ship.

John hugged his sister and said I will be here waiting until the steamer leaves. Rebecca left for the steamer while John was waiting and watching the last whistle of the departure.

The steamer whistled and moved on the seashore while John waiving his hands to his sister.

The steamer was slowly leaving the seashore while John was standing and watching the steamer disappear on the horizon. The foggy weather made John's eyes blurry to track the steamer.

John told his friend to go back to the horse carriage and drive to the village. It was almost late night when they arrived home late at night.

John told his wife Lucie about the long journey with his sister to the sea-shore. He also told his wife that Rebecca's visitation to the wealthy island would help them to get out from here.

He informed his wife that Rebecca stated "Lucie was kind to me while I was living in the house,"

"Lucie cried while her eyes were downcast"

"Why are you crying now?" John investigated.

"To be honest, I was not treated Rebecca nicely, I wish I would be able to bring her back home and treat her much better than ever, I kept making her do all the hard work at home, cleaning dishes, watering plants. She never dares to show no to me at all, she was very kind, nice, and patient in every way." Lucie explained.

"I know my sister is very kind and I could see that in her eyes, she would do the best to help us to overcome this difficult time, the Lord helps her to leave for a better place because she is in touch with our parents, she will be pleased with them and the Lord will be pleased with her," John commented.

He added "I always say my prayers and wish Rebecca had a wonderful journey to the island. I wish the weather condition remained stable for the next two weeks. If the weather condition remains stable for the next two weeks, the Queen Mary will arrive on time.

"Do not worry John about Rebecca; I am confident that she would be in good hands, and good future because she had a good heart" Lucie commented.

"I am really worried about the future of my sister;

I do not understand how those people are going to receive her.

I do not understand how those people are going to treat her.

I know that my sister needed to be happy and successful in the new land, but how does she manage and accustom to new life on the island, so many questions come into my mind while I was thinking of my sister." John puzzled.

Someday while I was thinking of Rebecca, the bell was ringing, birr-birr-birr, I picked up the phone,

"It is I, my brother John, I arrived safely and everything looks perfect," Rebecca's voice.

Wow! I was so impressed and thrilled to hear such good news from you Rebecca, here is Lucie wanted to talk to you on phone.

"How are you doing Rebecca?" Lucie inquired.

"Did you have a good journey?" Lucie asked.

"How did the islanders welcome you at the harbor? Lucie investigated.

"I had a very good journey, and Islanders welcomed me with great hospitality". Rebecca said.

"We have been talking about you, and even your friends in the countryside were asking about you."

John and I went to bed in a deep sleep and never open an eye all night.

Chapter 6

UNEXPECTED VISITOR

Lisa spent the rest of her life reading and writing books. She devoted much of her time working to improve the role of civil society organizations. She wrote three books related to the role of women in civil society. She read more than a thousand different books. She was very active in learning new things. She was very active in demonstrating application of theory to practice.

Lisa was busy at traveling to Denmark. She often travels to participate in meetings related to the role of civil society organizations.

The meetings were focusing on the role of civil society organizations in human rights around the world. She has been to Denmark many times. She loved to be there from time to time.

The government in Denmark implements judiciary laws that protect human rights in every way. The government also believes in transparency, accountability, and justice.

Lisa met with different participants in different meetings. The participants, whom Lisa met, believe in supporting human rights. She had become one of the ambassadors who function to raise awareness among people; she was becoming a member of several civic organizations in Africa and Asia.

Lisa believes that "education is a very important key that helps raise awareness among people; education is a key concept of enlisting the community that lacks knowledge. It makes people understand to live in peace and integrity, and promotes people to respect one another regardless of color, and ethnicity."

Education could make the ruler implement all the agenda that enrich the community potentially and successfully. Education could drive all people to work for the interest of their country.

While Lisa was in a meeting, she received a message from the captain of the Queen Mary. The captain confirmed to Lisa that Rebecca was on the ship heading to the Fertile Island. She will be there in a few days.

Lisa had already reserved an accommodation for Rebecca near a school. She also booked a tour bus for Rebecca to go up and down to identify the places on the island. In time, Rebecca would be able to enjoy watching the beauty of the island while touring up and down.

Lisa was also focusing on Denmark-island relationship" it was very interesting to see Lisa talking in detail about the strong relationship between the two countries. She was also pointing out that the relationship between two countries has also been growing more than ever before.

Lisa attended the meeting, and participated in it, and she submitted a proposal in the meeting. The proposal was talking about "globalization" the proposal has been reviewed and approved by most of the members of the meeting. The majority of the members of the meeting were very pleased that the proposal came from Lisa herself.

Lisa thanked the members of the meeting and left for the Fertile Island to complete the other project in relation to "welcome Rebecca." She would like to meet with Rebecca in person at the harbour.

Lisa had already talked to the English teacher Miss Havisham specialist in ESL Program. Miss Havisham was going to take care of Rebecca. She had been to Great Island many times and she knows English very well. In time, she has been selected by the Ministry of Education that she was the best English teacher on the island.

Lisa informed Miss Havisham that the newcomer Rebecca was on her way to the Fertile Island. Rebecca will be on the island within a week.

Miss Havisham had already prepared the course materials that fit the needs of her new student Rebecca.

She planned a head to talk to Rebecca upon her arrival. She was going to meet with Rebecca in the harbour and takes her to the boarding school.

Based on detailed information that Lisa had received from the villagers in the countryside, Rebecca had been to elementary school in the countryside for several years. She already knows Basic English but she doesn't know how to read well.

To prove that allegation, in the countryside Rebecca asked her brother John to read the letter that she found in the graveyard, John assisted and explained to Rebecca what the letter was talking about.

John studied English during his working days in the mines. There was a small English Centre opening on weekends. John grasped that opportunity and joined to learn English.

Miss Havisham would plan to qualify Rebecca to speak the language within a short period of time. She was going to focus on all English skills to help shaped Rebecca's ability in speaking English skills.

A week later, Lisa rang up Miss Havisham and asks why do not we meet and have lunch together someday next week? The time had come and both of them met together at the restaurant in down town. The restaurant's name is entitled: "enjoy food."

As Lisa and Miss Havisham were dining in the restaurant, they were sharing their preparation plan to welcome Rebecca. One of the most important things that they would do upon Rebecca's arrival is to come up with many islanders as possible for the harbour.

Islanders who work with Lisa had already designed their project to welcome Rebecca. They intended to welcome Rebecca with chanting words.

One day morning, the sky was mostly cloudy, rainy and the sun was a little bit shiny. The Queen Mary had just arrived at the harbour with a loud whistle. The moment that the Queen Mary stopped, the captain saw a large number of islanders at the harbour, they were raising the island flag and chanting:

Oh, island with followers and trees
Oh, island with dignity and treats
Oh, island with love and peace
Oh, the island welcomes Rebecca, please.

Rebecca did not show up for half an hour and Lisa was quite worried about the delay. Rebecca did not come out of the steamer on time. The islanders who were also there to welcome Rebecca were wandering about the delay; they kept asking one another about the delay.

Lisa was much respected in public because she used to work as a Queen of the island, she went and talked to the captain about Rebecca, but the captain told her that Rebecca has been detained inside the steamer by the custom-service, the reason because she did not have a valid document to enter the island.

Lisa told the attendees to be patient. She went inside the steamer and met with the custom service. She investigated with the custom services of Rebecca's document. Lisa respects the procedures of the entry visa to the island. She requested the custom services to take Rebecca's passport for renewal and return it.

The custom services respected Lisa's perspective. The customs services allowed Rebecca to accompany Lisa to the city, at the same time; Lisa would bring back the renewed passport to the customs services to issue the entry visa for Rebecca. Lisa thanked the custom-services for their understanding and cooperation.

After an hour of negation inside the steamer, Lisa and Rebecca came out of the steamer, while they were coming, they saw a large congregation of islanders chanting and waving their hands to Rebecca.

Rebecca was very excited to see islanders welcome her with cheers and love. Islanders throw followers on Rebecca as an expression of their love and peace.

Lisa introduced Miss Havisham to Rebecca as an English teacher. Lisa on behalf of Rebecca thanked all the presence for the social gathering at the harbour. In time, she invited all of them for dinner next week in the city hall as a symbol of peace and love.

Rebecca's arrival to the Fertile Island was a coincidence with the Christmas Eve celebration. Lisa invited all islanders to the city hall to celebrate, eat and dance for such a beautiful event.

A week later, Lisa and her friends organized a big event with a gigantic meal for all islanders. On that day, the weather was very nice. It was spring and you could see some clouds here and there in the sky. The weather was so great all day long.

The downtown was overcrowded with islanders who brought a lot of gifts to Rebecca. They all dressed up in new cloth. They dressed up in different colors that look as a rainbow.

Rebecca lives in a pretty sweet accommodation near the school. The accommodation was surrounded by a beautiful green fence. The ground was covered with thick green grass.

Rebecca found the accommodation includes a dining table, reading table, small library, and a living room with a big TV for watching the news, just to name a few.

Rebecca was studying English with some other international students have just arrived. She was going to enjoy learning English while interacting with other international students in the class.

Rebecca did not have to worry about food, because she was living in the boarding house, the boarding house provides Rebecca with free meals. These types of free services in the boarding house allow Rebecca to devote much of her time in studying.

She made some new friends in the classroom and spends much more time together speaking English café; Miss Havisham visits them in the boarding house quite often to join the English cafe.

They do watch some moves in English on weekends and write short reports about one of the movies that seem to be more important.

They do have a small English society that discussed different topics related to the significance of learning the language, each student should present a short topic in five minutes, and then the discussion followed to answer the difficult questions that required help from the teacher.

In the second session, Rebecca becomes very confident in speaking English and she went further and wrote short stories in relation to the countryside and discussed them with her classmates.

Everyone in the class believes that Rebecca was improving rapidly in English and within a few months, she is going to master the language skills with the help of Miss Havisham.

Rebecca has had rich information about the lifestyle in the countryside, and that countryside background enabling her to write different short stories in English and shared them with her classmates.

Miss Havisham encouraged Rebecca to keep writing such short stories on the school board, and later she could be able to collect all of them into a short booklet that could help make readers know much more about Rebecca's previous life.

At the end of the session, Rebecca wrote more than twenty different short stories about villagers' life in the countryside. One volunteer in the classroom stepped out and took permission from Rebecca to collect those short stories in a small booklet.

Miss Havisham wrote the introduction of the short booklet and brief information about the writer Rebecca.

The booklet had been published and become one of the popular booklets in the school library; Miss Havisham encouraged Rebecca to keep reading and writing skills from a different perspective.

A year later, the Ministry of Education requested that Rebecca introduce the booklet to the elementary school level.

The name of the booklet: **Storytellers in downtown.**

The booklet was talking about local islanders (youth and age). They would share stories about their life history of culture through a new vision. Islanders (youth and age) had already participated in the discussion.

Rebecca wanted to connect the countryside with islanders, so she decided to create such a space "**Storytellers in downtown.**" for participants who liked telling short stories about different events. She wanted to raise awareness among islanders who had a great history.

She intended to make the community a better place to live in.

"I was missing these storytelling series in such a unique conversation." Rebecca demonstrated. She added "Storytelling engagement associated with the city hall in downtown and a member of the storytelling from the other cities in the region.

Normally, local islanders would get together in person to learn from their elders in the downtown meeting every Sunday afternoon. Storytellers who work with the downtown aim to connect islanders to culture and the land through program of storytelling.

"Summer Stories: A time for listening, sharing, and connecting." Will be delivered in public town by elder islanders, and later the TV channels would show again the same program to islanders who would not have time to come in person downtown.

"It's all about connecting islanders to their land, sharing funny stories of the ancient time, legendries, and self-care. It feels like you are sitting in a circle with elders, that episode would help connect local islanders with beautiful stories from their communities, and also function as a learning opportunity for non-islanders.

"That was a great method of learning to engage in, everyone comes to watch and learn from elders because these teaching strategies apply to everyone who lives on the island.

"Winter Stories" is a collection of short and long stories made by collaboration between the storytellers who live on Fertile Island and the storytellers who live on the other islands.

Eight stories will be posted to a national article downtown, and also all these stories would be narrated on the TV channel at 8 p.m. on each of the following days: March 10, April 20, and May 27.

Dow-town looks vibrant with a variety of cultural programs that take place from time to time.

In summer, the island would become a place where islanders and non-islanders would find joy, peace, success, and happiness.

Miss Havisham was impressed by Rebecca's progress in school. She perceived Rebecca had strong writing skills in English as well as much interest in social studies.

Miss Havisham went through the booklet that has been written by Rebecca and commented on it, she mentioned in her commentary that the booklet is very interesting, touching and meaningful of short stories. It reflects the lifestyle of islanders and life style of the countryside where Rebecca has come from.

Miss Havisham delivered a long speech in the college about the importance of the booklet and how she could help to make it available for everyone in the market.

Miss Havisham suggested several social studies books for Rebecca to read. The books were talking about the role of social studies in progressive communities.

Miss Havisham raised several questions on the discussion table as below:

- Why do we concentrate on social studies at large?
- Do social studies assist poor communities to improve and developed?
- Is it important to do further studies in social studies to contribute to societies.

THE MINES

GOLG

SILVER

COPPER

BLACK GOLD

NATURAL GAS

Chapter 7

THE MINES

Rose was well-connected with the king of the Great Island.
She sent a weekly report in detailed information to the king.

The report was about the economic sources in all islands. She also provided the King with a map of all locations of the wealth in the region.

She also informed the king that all Queens in different islands have fully collaborated with their weekly reports. On top of that, she sent a video cassette to the king about the national day including the Queens' photo sitting next to Rose.

She also sent a video cassette to the king demonstrates some images of other Queens were submitting reports to Rose. Rose receives weekly reports from all islands. She thanked all Queens for their confidential work. She kept recommending them to be careful while they were collecting or sending reports about the economic resources in the islands.

Rose arranged a gigantic meal for the Queens. She invited all of them to the palace for a dinner table. While they were dining, they were talking about their plan and how they could work professionally and potentially together.

The king told Rose some of his commanders would visit the wealthy location on the island. They would visit confidentially the wealthy location to loot some gold. Rose agreed and advised the commanders to visit the wealthy island on the national day.

All islanders on that day would be busy at the national day celebration and might not pay attention to border security. She recommended commanders to be careful during their visit. However, if islanders see strangers on the island, they will inform the Queen.

The king was glad at having Rose on the island as an evil plan. The king sent a helicopter with some commanders on the national day to dig the wealth on the island.

The king communicated with the commanders to be cautious on that day and also to be well-prepared for any possible action. He also advised them to be friendly with islanders; he also advised them not to talk to islanders if they approach and ask questions.

Islanders began to be curious about knowing strangers in their land with such a huge helicopter. A helicopter perhaps it has come from a foreign country with seven commanders on it. They have owned advanced equipment. The equipment helps them to identify the location of the wealth.

ONE EVENING ABOUT A YEAR AGO, a group of islanders made a short trip to the small island about 80 miles from the Centre of the town. That small island was an island devoid of islanders. But it is rich in natural resources, such as gold, silver, monomers, copper, and uranium. It is an island that belongs to the administration of the government.

The island is very rich. It covered with green grass. It has several wild animals. The animals were roaming in groups after groups across the island. Most of the animals were friendly to islanders.

On weekends, islanders go visit an island that is full of flowers, and trees. They like watching waterfalls on low lands and high lands. They would prefer to visit the island on weekends because they could be able to relax and be away from working hours.

The government does not prohibit its islanders from trips and entertainment parties on the island. The authority would love to perceive them visiting the island and spend a good time together.

A year ago, a group of islanders went to the island and spent a good time together with their families. They usually camp in the Centre of the island. They would prefer to camp in the Centre of the island because they could be able to walk and visit all parts of the island. There were several waterfalls in the Centre. That was one of the causes for choosing the Centre. They usually camp near the waterfalls. In summer the waterfall reduces heat in the place where islanders were camping.

ONE DAY EVENING, SOME ISLANDERS WERE WALKING ACROSS THE ISLAND.

While they were walking up and down the island, they saw a helicopter landing on the low land behind some tall green grass; they also saw five smugglers beyond the helicopter digging in the ground. They also saw five smugglers packing gold into small boxes; they also noticed two other smugglers placing boxes in the helicopter. They also saw a huge amount of gold piles in big boxes. More importantly, they even saw fire sticks as well.

Some smugglers were using some machines to dig down in the ground when it was hard to dig it out. They blew it out with the fire sticks. They avoid blowing the rock with the fire sticks. They apply fire-sticks when it was hard to dig them out.

Smugglers never dare to draw attention of the islanders to what they were doing. As soon as islanders were approaching, they stopped digging and got on the helicopter. Islanders just ignored them and kept on moving up and down the hilly areas on the island.

One of the islanders was getting mad at smugglers "look, those smugglers had come from somewhere to our island to take our wealth," he added that "look the mines, and the rest of the islanders were "shouting" very angrily with those smugglers who come from somewhere to steal our wealth. "We needed to be vigilant and alert our government instantly about this event.

"No one was expecting to see a helicopter landing on our wealthy island. Smugglers come from somewhere and obtained a huge amount of gold and leave." One islander commented.

One eyewitness of the islander noted "I was getting much angrier when I perceived a helicopter landing on the island." He added "I saw the smugglers whispering to one another while they were blowing the rocks.

"It was not hard to reach the wealth on this island," because the wealth is so near to the surface of the ground. It was very easy to dig a little bit and get gold or other natural resources." One smuggler mentioned to his co-worker.

While a group of islanders was returning to their camp. A helicopter flies over the island. Some other islanders also saw a helicopter landing. They saw it landing behind the mountain.

There were two geologists' Mr. George, and Mr. Bill. They both have had much information about the mines. They both graduated from the Institute of Geology, they have been working in the mines for several years. They have come to know the smugglers were prospectors and technicians. They come from somewhere to smuggle wealth.

Let us listen to the following conversation between Bill and George.

What they were talking about:

"What would you do George?" Bill said.

"We should inform our government upon arrival home," George responded.

Would you be able to guess from where those smugglers" Bill asked?

"Perhaps they have come from a foreign country."

"I think so, they have come from the Great Island," Bill said.

"You know George when the helicopter was taking off, it flew over our heads, it flew very close to the surface of the land. In time, I looked up and noticed the written capital letters G.I.in white on the frame of the helicopter". Bill told.

What? George inquired.

"While a helicopter was taking off, I saw a written capital letters G.I. in white color on the frame of the helicopter," Bill confirmed.

Wow! "Those two big capital letters G.I. in white could stand for "Great Island" George commented.

"Yes, indeed, I have had proof for that; I took a snapshot with my camera to proof the image of the helicopter while it was taking off. I know that when you talk about such a sensitive issue like this you need to show evidence," Bill mentioned.

"Would you like to go with me to the Queen?" Bill asked.

Yes. I will do it gladly; we needed to show our patriotism to the Queen by monitoring our wealth on the island and informing the Queen of any suspicious movements in places of natural wealth. Additionally, if we do this, we will preserve our wealth from plunder.

AT THREE O'CLOCK IN THE EVENING, BILL AND GEORGE RETURN ED HOME. From there both of them went to the palace to meet with the Queen. In the palace, they first met with the director of the Queen's office Miss Rose. She told them that the Queen was in a meeting with some guests.

How could I help you? Rose asked.

They say, they wanted to meet with the Queen in person because they had brought confidential information.

She argued with them that, she would be able to convey the message to the Queen, but the two gentlemen insisted on meeting with the Queen in person because the issue seems to be important.

Would you please tell me in brief what is the matter? Rose asked.

They told Rose about what had happened on the island along with the proof of an image of a helicopter.

Rose stated that "such an issue was not necessary to be presented to the Queen; I would take care of it by myself." But the two gentlemen were insisting on meeting with the Queen. While they were arguing with Rose, the Queen came out of the meeting on time.

As the Queen was coming out of the meeting, she saw Rose with two gentlemen talking to one another. The Queen went right away to the gentlemen and listened to their story. The gentlemen immediately informed the Queen about the profile in detailed information; they also showed the Queen some images related to the helicopter while flying over the island.

What did Rose say about this sensitive profile? The Queen inquired.

"I am Rose; I would take care of such an issue and was not necessary to be presented to the Queen." Gentlemen repeated what Rose had said to them.

"The issue is dangerous, and impermissible at the same time, it is an impermissible invasion of our borders. She added that "this behaviour was impermissible in a conservative society" We needed to be strong and vigilant in terms of our national security. However "The helicopter belongs to the Great Island, and that based on the image of the helicopter and the abbreviation of capital letters G.I. in white color." The Queen spoke.

The Queen scheduled a private meeting with the gentlemen at 10: 00 AM. The Queen wanted the two gentlemen to join her intelligence team on the island.

In the morning at ten, the Queen met with the gentlemen in her private office, they discussed that profile in detail. She thanks the two gentlemen for their concerns about the safety of the island.

She requested the two gentlemen to join the government team in national security. They agreed to work undercover and to submit daily reports directly to the Queen.

The Queen also held an emergency meeting with the security forces and discussed the formation of a high committee headed by the Supreme Commander of the Armed Forces, Mr. Dan. The high committee visited the island, reviewed the security situation and submitted a report to the prime minister about the amount of the looted gold. A high committee took serious measures to prevent the recurrence of the event.

Three days later, the specialized committee looked at the security situation on the island and come up with the following detailed information:

- The event of the smuggling of gold from the island coincided with the islanders' preoccupation with the celebration of the national day.
- The amount of stolen gold was estimated to be approximately nine hundred billion dollars.

In the meantime, the Cabinet reviewed the security report and issued the following decisions:

- Deploying a security unit to monitor the island throughout the week, in rotation with the members of security unit.
- Submitting a weekly report to the security authorities about the situation in the island

KEEP

IN

MIND

ROSE

WORKS

FOR

CENTRAL

INTELLIGENCE

BUREAU

IN

THE

GREAT

ISLAND

Chapter 8

C.I.B.PLAN

THE INVESTIGATION OF THE GOVERNMENT IN THE FERTILE ISLAND CONFIRMED that the military plane belongs to the Great Island.

The radio FM Island and TV channels were talking about the violation of the island's wealth. Islanders reacted aggressively and marched a rally down the road. They condemned the violation of the island's wealth. They asked the government to take necessary measures to protect the island's wealth. They claimed the government to identify the smugglers and bring them to justice.

The Queen was shocked to hear about the event. She urgently met with islanders in downtown and promised to investigate and bring the criminals to justice.

The islanders acknowledged the Queen for the strong message and they repeatedly asked her to take serious measures to get the criminals to justice. The rally was continuing for three days across the island, some islanders met with the Queen in person to investigate the event.

The Queen convinced the islanders that she would do whatever she can to find out who was behind the act and brings him to justice.

Additionally, the international organizations and regional organizations also condemned the violation of the Wealthy Island and they encouraged the government to take serious action against criminals who landed on the island and smuggled its wealth.

A helicopter landed in the afternoon, the weather forecast was foggy, and smugglers had a map to help them find the place where gold is available on the surface of the ground.

Smugglers were delighted to have had a map that made their task much easier and achievable; smugglers spent only three hours on the island and managed within that short time to collect a huge amount of gold.

Most smugglers were surprised at finding a huge amount on the surface of the ground, they had advanced dedicative machines support them to track the natural resources on the ground.

On the other hand, the king of the Great Island declared his support for the island to protect its wealth from outsiders. At the same time, the Queen of the island sent a strong message to the king expressing her gratitude, she added, "the island does not ask for help. The island has a big army on active duty."

The king sent a warship with military force to examine the situation on the island, when the warship arrived near the port of the island, the maritime authorities prevented it from entering the port.

After that, the warship returned to the Great Island unsuccessfully, and the King of the Great Island declared war, a week later, the relationship between the two islands collapsed.

The king failed to convince the Queen about his plan. The Queen strongly condemned the idea of letting a warship stay at the port even for a while.

A week later, the Queen talked on TV channels and informed islanders that the helicopter belongs to the Great Island. The Queen had proof that the smugglers who invaded the wealthy island from the Great Island,

The Queen was going to study this event with the commanders of the army. She was also going to study it with the government members to take action that would please islanders. She added, "That any person who dares to enter our territory would be accounted."

"Our message to worldwide that we have to protect our land, islanders and wealth, we, islanders were born to live on this land, love it and die for it," Islanders confirmed.

"We, islanders have had our natural resources, we developed our land by our islanders, we built our land by our labors and we, islanders have had a unique governing system that made all of us equal before laws," Islanders declared.

"We, islanders, we do not have had a social discrimination or segregation, we all equal before laws, we all share our job opportunities that based on professionalism and patriotism." Islander believed.

Islanders added that "Today, we, islanders needed to be in unity more than ever before, our wealthy island was facing a problem from the outsiders who plan day and night to invade. We needed to be vigilant to protect our natural resources that made us live in peace, love, and dignity.

We do not need someone else from somewhere to come and give us advice or humiliate our lives, to be safe please everyone needs to do his part and we islanders would win to defeat the enemy."

"We, islanders, have had all institutions here on the island, we have had all experts here on the island, we have had all our advanced technology and advanced institutions in all walks of life.

We just needed to collaborate and prepared ourselves at all times particularly in this unprecedented time, to avoid contradictions and predictions, we always need to stand for on guard to defend our land." Islanders said.

"We, islanders, have had a big army that prepared for necessity, we do not interest in war, but if we face war, we will react immediately to protect our land. We delivered this strong message to the nation that we, islanders decided to stand up for guard our land." Islanders decided.

"We, islanders already have received support from all over the world to take any necessary action to protect our land from invasion. It was quite interesting to see all nation steps out and rejected the idea of humiliation, discrimination, and violation.

We, islanders, understand the international laws that allow us to do whatever we can to stop invaders. Yes, indeed, the law is above all, the law is considered to be our torch to stop crimes in the present times." Islanders thought.

In general, the government in the island takes responsibility for issues impact on the island. These include the island protection, forcign policy and national security.

The island is a democracy. But most of the countries in different parts of the world were governing by authoritarian regimes. These regimes use their power to invade islands that have a system of parliamentary government.

The fact that islands have commitment to social justice and respect everyone's rights, while authoritarian regime disagrees with, basic freedoms, such as freedom of thought and freedom of speech.

Chapter 9

DO YOU REMEMBER REBECCA?

If you do not remember Rebecca, it doesn't matter. I will remind you again. It was a story of an orphan girl. The story of Rebecca seems to be important in the scene, Rebecca used to live in the countryside. But now she lives on Fertile Island.

Upon her arrival on the island, Rebecca had been welcomed by large numbers of islanders and being offered a space to live, and school to learn the language.

Rebecca has been learning English and French for three years at the college of languages. After a few years, she was joining social studies at the University of Island. She had been to France more than three times. She has been there for practicing French conversational skills.

Rebecca attained a Bachelor of Arts honours in social studies from the Island University. She becomes famous for dancing during her school days. She participated in different cultural programs at schools. She also won many prizes in school.

She was also working with Lisa on the community culture at the city hall. Lisa allows her to organize several cultural programs related to culture folks and diverse communities. Lisa encourages Rebecca to become the organizer of all programs in the community.

Rebecca organizes programs related to community development to help people by combating homelessness and offering food to community issues. Over the past two years, Rebecca works closely with hundreds of homeless and low-income members in different countries. She continued working to support people who face financial difficulties.

How did Rebecca become confident in her work?

Rebecca becomes confident at work because Lisa encouraged her to involve in any single workplace that is related to the community. Lisa's teaching strategies enabled Rebecca to gain much more knowledge in the workplace.

Rebecca becomes one of the most famous ladies in social activities across the islands. She visits all islands and participates in social and cultural programs; she received many rewards and recognitions from civil society organizations.

Rebecca utilized her school days in studying and participating in social activities at large. She has been known by most islanders on islands. She was very generous and kind in every way. She made a lot of friends on islands as well.

She usually works as a volunteer in the community on vacations; she sometimes works to help sick people to get well. She becomes a problem solver and public speaker. She creates and maintains social work environment. She organized a social program for elders in the city by inviting actors and singers on the stage.

Rebecca's English teacher Miss Havisham had been sick on bed for a while. She had a severe fever and cough for a while. Rebecca was becoming extremely busy working at the

Community Centre. She did not know that Miss Havisham is sick on a bed.

Miss Havisham knows that Rebecca is so busy working in the community, however, she does not want Rebecca knows that she is seriously ill. At the same time, Lisa was in touch with Miss Havisham from time to time.

One evening at about seven o'clock, Rebecca received a call from Lisa was saying "that Miss Havisham had passed away. Tomorrow the funeral would take place at the last resting place; Rebecca was very sad deep to miss her teacher during that time.

The next day morning, islanders gathered at the funeral place and paid their last respect to the funeral. They placed flowers on the coffin. They mentioned good deeds that were achieved by Miss Havisham during her school days.

Rebecca delivered an impressive speech full of love and respect for Miss Havisham, indicating that islanders will never forget Miss Havisham devoted much of her time teaching at the college for years and years. She pointed out: "Employees in the public or private sector had been students in Miss Havisham's class."

Rebecca opened "a community Centre of remembrance Miss Havisham" Islanders endorsed the new Community Centre will be a center of remembrance for Miss Havisham's contribution. Rebecca has become well-known and respected in all walks of life.

The Ministry of education had also established a university in the name of "Miss Havisham's University;" the University has three departments,

- The department of languages and cultures,
- The department of science,
- The department of social studies.

Lisa informed islanders that Miss Havisham wrote a booklet about her school days, [Rebecca School days] she mentioned in it the beauty of the island and islanders in spring. The book is available in the library for all islanders.

"I read it I enjoyed it and I encourage everyone to read it," Lisa said.

The Department of languages would print the booklet of Miss Havisham and distribute it free of charge to all islanders because Miss Havisham had been teaching in the department for more than thirty years.

A year later, Rebecca had been promoted in her job to become the general director of all civil society organizations in the region. Rebecca was not very much interested in becoming a big bossy; she thought wrongly that she was still younger to take over a general director. However, Lisa motivated Rebecca to accept the position.

Lisa has been working closely with Rebecca for several years; she knows that Rebecca could do the job efficiently. Lisa went further and convinced Rebecca to travel together whenever necessary to meet with other intellectual people internationally.

Lisa had a plan to push Rebecca later into another high position. The time will tell. The position is entitled the general secretary of the United Nations (U.N). The time has come and Lisa recommended Rebecca to be the head of the United Nations for several considerations:

- Rebecca had much more information about the role of the UN
- Rebecca achieved two degrees, one in social studies and the other one in international law.
- She had developed and maintained friendly relationships with other people due to her strong interpersonal skills and approachability.

Rebecca accompanied Lisa several times to Denmark to attend the international conference. The conference discusses the role of international organizations in the area where the abuse of women's rights is still alive and kicking.

Lisa was impressed by Rebecca's speech in one of the conferences related to human's rights. Rebecca spoke out for an hour in detailed information about what they could do as organizations to help shape the affected areas across the globe. She spoke for half an hour in English and half an hour in French. Everyone applauded when Rebecca sat down.

Mr. Speaker commented on Rebecca's speech "That was a very informative speech we have not heard before since the formation of these organizations" he added, "we needed such a young generation to lead because leadership requires talent, patience, and motivation."

Lisa met with Asia and told her in detail about the significance of leadership roles in promoting professional training at all workplaces.

In this regard, Lisa convinced the Queen to support Rebecca to become the head of the United Nations. The Queen was very pleased that the idea of supporting Rebecca to become the head of UN Office comes from Lisa herself.

One evening, While Rebecca was sitting next to Lisa watching tv news, she saw lightning passes through the window. She stood up and went outdoors and looked up in the sky.

Lisa followed Rebecca but she did not interrupt her while she was looking up in the sky, after a moment,

"What was happening" Lisa inquired.

"I am extremely concerned about our future," Rebecca responded.

Rebecca remembers her parents buried in the graveyard,
Rebecca remembers her brother lives in poverty
Rebecca remembers her promise to the villagers
Rebecca remembers her childhood in the village

Rebecca talked to Lisa about her brother John and how much he suffers in the countryside. She wanted to help him. In the meantime, she wants to ask Asia if she could allow her to bring him here.

Rebecca gets permission from the Queen to bring her brother to the Fertile Island. She offers Rebecca unlimited authority to help more than ten people to move from the countryside and live on island.

Rebecca thanked the Queen for the offer and promised to utilize the authority in good manners; Rebecca went to the countryside along with Lisa for a week's trip. She met with all villagers. She met with her brother John and his wife as well.

She found John had two twins, and he was so happy working in the mines to feed them. He was looking a little bit tired and weak from overwork. She told him that she works for the government in a high position. She added that "the time has come to pay back to assist John and the villagers,

Firstly, she went to the graveyard to meet with her parents and put flowers on their graves. She thanks them for everything they did to make her life much easier.

Secondly, she opened two high schools in the countryside, one for girls and one for boys. She opened a new community Centre for villagers to spend a good time together and socialize with one another.

Rebecca's visitation bridges the gap between Fertile Island and the countryside. The visitation helps Rebecca to understand the similarities and differences between one culture and another. The visitation helps Rebecca to get experience from the whole places where she had been to.

Rebecca becomes famous for revisiting the village and meeting with villagers in the country. She helps improve the housing condition that the majority of villagers live in and doubles the amount of housing that is now available.

Rebecca's visitation helps shape the lifestyle of villagers and motivates them to change their way of life. Rebecca encourages villages to send their children to school. She confirms school opens great opportunities to children in the future. It seems to be important that school creates job opportunities for learners. In particular, when children grew up, they would visit other countries to look for further studies.

Thirdly, Rebecca gave John one thousand dollars to clear his entire debt. She asked him to be prepared and leave for the Fertile Island. In time, Rebecca wanted also to support villagers to live the best life. She wanted to build more schools, community centers, and hospitals in the countryside.

John decided to sell his house and the farm, Rebecca "It is better to discuss this issue with your wife,

"Keep the house and allows someone from your old friends to live in it and take care of it. You never know, someday, somewhere we may revisit the countryside. Then we have a home to live in," Lucie suggested.

Rebecca says, to John "Someone will see you next week." He will give you some tickets and take you to the same place where I left for the island.

I will be leaving in the morning to Europe to attend a conference n Denmark.

Do not worry about expenses for your transportation; all travel expenses will not be serious. I just wanted you to go shopping for your trip and do not forget to invite all villagers for dinner before you leave.

Lisa and I will be waiting for you at the port. Do not be surprised if you see hundreds and hundreds of islanders waiting in line. They will be waiting to greet you.

A week later, Rebecca's family arrived at the port. It was a sunny day and the weather was very moderate, a vast majority of islanders were waiting at the seashore to welcome Rebecca's family. While the family was coming out of the steamer, islanders were chanting with warm hospitality.

The family loved the island and its islanders, the family also liked their new townhouse that was surrounded by a green-lawn yard that had everything in it. The family had a good impression of the way they have been received at the port.

Rebecca encouraged John to go to school, but he was not very motivated. He thought he is old to go to school. She convinced him to do a diploma in tourism so that he could work in some international hotels downtown.

Successfully, he joined the College for two years program with a diploma in tourism. After graduation, he got a job opportunity as an assistant in one of the international hotels downtown. A year passed; he had been promoted and become the hotel manager.

Lucie has twins made her busy enough. She preferred to be a housewife and takes care of the twins. John works as a hotel manager. Lucie believes that John has enough salary to bring food to the table.

Lucie helps John to save some money for emergencies and other troubles. They both live a happy life on the island. They do not have problems worrying about the school expenditures for their twins when they grow up, and they are thrilled to save enough money for their twins to go to school.

One of the great things is that John did not forget his old friend James. James lives in the countryside; he talks to him on phone and provides him with some financial assistance.

John kept calling James and asking about the land and the housing condition. John and his wife decided to revisit the countryside; James told them the house was in good condition.

He also told him that the agricultural land is being cultivated for crops this year because of the heavy rain; he expects a lot of grains at the end of the harvest session. He added, "I have a good surprise for you when you come." John was curious about the surprise, but his friend refused to disclose it on the phone.

Chapter 10

JOHN REVISITS A COUNTRYSIDE

Ten years have passed, John revisited the countryside and met with his old friends, he was very happy to meet again with his friends.

He went with his wife to be connected with the countryside.

He went with his wife to be remembered by his friends.

He went with his wife to recall the past.

He went with his wife to fulfill the promise that he already made.

John and Lucie arrived in the countryside on Monday early morning. It was autumn, the sky was blue and covered with dark clouds. The wind blows and shakes the leaves on the trees gently. The ground was covered with green grass.

Birds chirp on trees, on land, in fields and fly everywhere; water was gushing out from high land to low land, wild animals gathering round the spring to drink and swim.

John and Lucie were thrilled to revisit the countryside in autumn. The only thing that was bothering them in autumn was a mosquito, mosquitos in places of stagnant water swamps.

John went to the countryside to revisit his old townhouse. He met with his old friend Mr. James. James was the housekeeper of it. John found it in good condition because James did many renovations to keep it in good shape.

James installed new windows and replaced all furniture in the living room. He also bought new carpets, tea-table for the balcony and bedrooms.

John asked: where did you get the money?

James says to John: "You know, when you left me to take care of the house and the land, I cultivated the land more than three times and made a lot of money from the land. I saved five thousand for you in the bank and that money for you."

He added, "I have more than ten thousand dollars in my bank account, all that money I got from my work on the farm."

"I am so happy to hear that, and I just wanted to let you know that I have become richer than ever before. I do not want that money you had saved. If you need it, please keep it," John responded.

Villagers organized a farewell party for John and Lucie. They even invited all neighboring friends to join the party. It was a great moment for them to meet with all villagers; it was also an opportunity for them to meet with their old friends and siblings.

Villagers cooked different kinds of delicious food; all who were at the farewell party very contented and satisfied with the food. John grasped that opportunity and thanked all of his friends for their coming. As he was talking, tears running down his face.

John had an old friend name, Abel. He lives in the countryside. He was a shoemaker. He had a small shop in the market. He was making new shoes for men and women. He was also fixing broken shoes with little money. He had many customers. He works five days a week.

Abel helped John many times to mend his broken- shoes. It was happening when John used to work in the mines. Abel refuses many times to charge John for that little work. Abel kept telling John this proverb "A friend in need is a friend indeed."

"From where did you learn this good proverb?" John asked.

"I have just learned it from a tourist who comes from the Great Island," Abel answered.

"Did you remember his name?" John inquired.

"Yes, indeed, his name is Peter," Abel answered.

"Why did foreigners come to the countryside? John investigated.

"You know, a long time ago, tourists would not like to come here because of the bad weather, water, and food, but now due to climate change, the countryside looks better than ever," Abel said.

He added, "Now the news started talking about the beauty of the countryside, that type of advertisement drew the attention of a tourist to come and enjoy the beauty of the weather here in the countryside."

"They come to the countryside to spend a good time with ordinary people. They usually like the spring to enjoy the beauty of the green land," Abel commented.

In spring, the trees in the countryside blossom and show up their colors, red, white, yellow, brown, and green.

That was a meaningful conversation between John and Abel in the old time when the time was becoming memories. He never forgets that moment forever, now the right time has come to bring John back to the countryside for a short period to pay back to the villagers.

While John was talking to someone at the party, he remembered his old friend Abel. He wanted to see his old friend Abel. He wanted to reward him, but John did not see

Abel at the party, he asked about Abel, but the villager told him that Abel had passed away three years ago.

John burst into tears because he missed his old friend, Abel, he wanted to please him, but unfortunately, he was not there anymore. Villagers stand with John and support him during that sad moment.

John planned to take Abel with him to the island forever; Abel had no children or family anymore in the countryside. He was living by himself in a beautiful house; the community leader found a letter in the mailbox from Abel indicating that "when I die, use my house as a Community Centre for villagers."

The community leader took the letter from the mailbox. He invited all villagers to a large congregation and read the letter out. Villagers thanked Abel so much for his kindness. They stood up for a moment of respect to Abel who had already surprised them with his good deeds.

It was a historical moment when John and Lucie visited Abel's graveyard and put some roses in it. They offered supplications and prayers and told him they would not forget him to revisit.

John revisited the countryside and managed to meet with all his friends. He perceived that everything in the village was developed and improved for better and better.

It was shocking for villagers to see John and Lucie in the marshes. They put some flowers and offered prayers for them; they also managed to support villagers and donated funds to the community charity.

John donated his old house and the farm to the community charity and raised some funds to build a medical clinic for the villagers. He also trained some nurses on the island with medical tools monthly from the Fertile Island.

John and Lucie wanted to give back to the community where they grew up, that was their plan ten years ago, and the time has come to put it into practice through the actual revisit and donation for their generation.

John was amazed and impressed by the changes that had already been taking place in the countryside. He saw new roads, schools, and two colleges, one college for academic education and one for technical education, and he also noticed a new big hospital in the countryside.

He was also astonished to acknowledge the Faculty of Agriculture receives international students to study soil and agriculture. He found a lot of new extension land for plantations. He also saw new extension areas with social services.

The colleges have accommodations for international students. John met with many students in the college cafeteria and asked them about their impressions of the countryside. Most students informed John that the great lady Rebecca built all these institutions ten years ago.

All villagers knew Rebecca very well, some villagers believed that she used to live in the countryside, but she does not live here anymore, and perhaps she lives in another country. But based on recent detailed Rebecca lives on Fertile Island, everybody knows that island is very rich in every way, and everyone who lives in the countryside dreams of someday moving to Fertile Island.

When John and Lucie left the countryside, it was in a bad situation, with nothing to entice the eyes. As they returned, things had changed for the better. The lowlands and high lands covered with rich grass.

They found all places where villagers lived were becoming tidy. They also found new roads, schools, hospitals, and colleges, just to name a few. They kept asking villagers about the person who brought the change.

They get to know from villagers in town that Rebecca helps shape the countryside. Rebecca works actively with other professional volunteers to make this social change happen.

Students learned from Rebecca that there are so many job opportunities on the island. After graduation, they can have opportunities to work on the island. Rebecca encourages students to achieve academic qualifications because the island requires professional people to contribute to the community at large.

After graduation, students plan to go and work on the Fertile Island; we do not know if we can make it, but we will see later what the future brings for us, hoping that Rebecca will be in a position to help them.

John thanked all the students in the cafeteria and left with a very good impression of his sister Rebecca, but he did not tell them that Rebecca is his sister.

In the evening, John went with Lucie to the hospital for a visit, and they found the hospital in the name of Rebecca. They were shocked to see the name of Rebecca inaugurated on a big piece of stone, it was written on the stone the name of the hospital and the donator's name that was Rebecca, and the year of establishment.

They had been in the countryside for fifteen days; the days passed quickly, and they were enjoyable and lovely. The days were full of memories and joy. They might never do it again. But they remain and last in their brains.

Ten years have passed, with many changes ever last

Ten years have passed, and become memories last

Ten years have passed; John revisits a country at last

Ten years have passed, and Rebecca's name remains as a remark

Chapter 11

AN ADVENTURE ONE

People in the countryside had received John with great pleasure and happiness. He told villagers about the standard of living on the island.

And how much does he love living on the island?

Some villagers love to change their lifestyle for the better, and they start thinking of an adventure someday somewhere. They heard about many people who travel to the island for several reasons. For example, some travel to explore new places, and some travel to look for a job.

Youth have decided that now is the time for travel. Firstly, they do not know how to travel and where to go. They start studying ways of travel. They agreed to travel on land. They collected detailed information to guide them to their destination.

Once upon a time, some teenagers held a meeting and decided to travel by small boat to the Fertile Island. They prepared their food and drinking water to support them survives for a month. They made their boat from the bushes near the sea. It took them twenty days to be built and go on an exciting adventure.

It was summer, the weather forecast was mild, and nothing happened to them at all. They know how to swim, but they do not know how to read a map. They did not tell their parents in the countryside that they were planning to adventure to their final destination.

In the summer afternoon, they got into a boat and started paddling on the sea. They have a small compass to show them directions and a small map of where to go.

They were six young men in the boat who prepared a unique schedule for them to paddle the boat. They divided the duties into three work shifts. Two persons work in the mornings, two persons work in the afternoons, and two persons work late at night.

They started the journey in the afternoon. It was a nice weather when the boat was sailing on the sea. While waves were rolling behind waves, they were happily singing and dancing.

These young men decided to adventure with the ambition to strive for a better place where "education and job opportunities are available for everyone in the rich island."

But they might not think that what they were doing was illegal for leaving their village. They might not think of their land that is richer than many other places.

Jack is one of the boys on the boat who knows directions and maps well. He studied maps at the university, at it, he learned a lot about maps and forecasts. He devoted much of his time guided the boat in the right direction.

They have been sailing on the sea for more than twenty days. During that time, the weather was quiet, and nothing happened to them. Sometimes they get some rest and look for the seashore to get some food and drinking water, as they were sailing on a boat; they came across a small village. Villagers were so kind to provide them with food and water.

At night, the young boys were lying on their backs on the boat. While they were sailing, waves were rolling behind waves. It was a quiet night with bright stars twinkling in the sky.

The journey took several days to the Fertile Island. The Fertile Island is their final destination. Their time was enjoyable and passed quickly because of the good weather forecast.

On the tenth night, they passed some places where a huge rock and water lilies caused some difficulties in sailing at night, but they managed to paddle through the water plants.

After dark every night, they passed a small town, just a shine of lights. On the twelfth night, they slipped to the seashore to get supplied with food and some drinking water.

One of them gets sick on the boat. Their friends brought him to the village for medical treatment, took him to the small hospital in the town, and left. The doctor did some blood work for him.

The next day, the doctor told Dave that his health condition was stable and now you are free to leave the hospital, he found out that his friends had already left the seashore.

Dave was twenty years old; he was a clever boy. He went downtown to get some help. While he was walking by the side of the road, he saw a man sitting on the ground. He went and asked him if he needed help. The man said yes,

Would you please take me to my home?
Here is my home address written on this envelope.
34 Banner Street, Shiny town, CA, N3M 2E9.

"Today I have a headache and stomach ache. I saw the doctor last week. He advised me not to drive anymore because I have a vision problem. I do not have a younger brother to take care of me. I am a rich man and own a big house. I came to the hospital on foot this morning. The weather was good in the morning.

It took me an hour walking to get to the hospital. But now I am not in good health condition to walk.

Would you please call a city cab? The man requested.

The boy did call the city cab. The taxi driver would be there within 20 minutes because the main road was closed because of an accident.

Dave was also lucky to find a man on the street; he helps Dave at the same time to get a place to sleep for the night.

On the other hand, Jack looked at the map "I believe three more nights would bring us to the harbor of the Fertile Island, where we would leave the boat and swim to the harbor."

Jack added, "At the harbor, many steamboats were staying when they were not traveling, we easily could find one of them and get into it, and then we would be out of trouble."

On the 25th night a heavy mist and cloudy sky in the morning, but there was no strong wind; they were talking about the identification of Fertile Island. They wondered if they would be able to identify the location of the island.

Jack said, "There was to pay attention to the location; the island had a tall tower decorated with lights at night."

While the boat was sailing, Dave jumped up and said that light would be a tower of the island, "But it was not, that to be a moving light of some insects flying around in the seashore," Jack responded.

"Look over there, now that light was the light of the tower of the island at last," Someone said.

"You are right! It is the tower light,"

"We are safe in a good place now. The boat moves slowly towards the seashore where maybe the security guard was watching us from so far while we were approaching steamboats," Jack said.

"I will tell you what to do now, leave everything on the boat and jump into the water and swim towards that steamboat as fast as possible and do not listen to any person who would try to hinder you from swimming to the shore, three, two, one, jump off," jack ordered.

Jack was the best swimmer among them, he reached the seashore, and the sea guard arrested Jack. He informed the sea guard about his friends who were swimming against the current of the water.

They were getting tired because of the waves and the cold wind. The sea guard was searching for the rest of the boys, and after half an hour of searching, they found them all clung to a floating wood.

They have been driven to the seashore safely by the sea guard.

Jack was the first one who successfully reached the seashore safely without help. Jack was upset and looked at the sea angrily "You swallowed my friends," I should inform their families and never again on small boats to young generations who would attempt to imitate us."

The security took them to the immigration office for investigation, then they took them to the hospital for a medical check-up, and then after that, they sent them back to the place where they could have some rest and food.

The sea guard informed Jack that all his friends in good health now, in the meantime, boys must be place in different places for a while. The security separated them from one another for the trial and investigation.

The security wanted to investigate them individually to ensure that they had good records and what they would tell individually correct.

The security wanted them to swear to tell the truth and nothing but the truth before they settled down on the Fertile Island.

After a week, Jack had sent to court for a trial, and the court raised the following questions:

Why did you enter the island?
How did you enter the island?
With whom do you enter the island?

Jack answered all the questions raised by the court, and eventually he had given citizenship of the island. He has accepted to live happily as a new islander.

The court asked Jack's friends the same questions, and the court found out that they all were telling the same story and answers, and the immigration office court understood that all boys had come to the island looking for a better life. They all have become new islanders.

Jack went to school for three years, and he learned within three years English, and then after that, he did a diploma in information technology for three years too. He learned a lot about Microsoft Office.

He joined a great company for business and worked as a clerk for three years. He gained some work experience in computers. He decided to do some further studies in Computer Engineering. He applied for it, and he did not get it.

He changed his mind and worked for the Petroleum Exploration Company for several years. He decided to revisit his parents in the countryside. He made a lot of money on the island a long time ago. Now he is eligible to bring his parents in if he would like.

Jack had direct contact with his elder brother in the countryside, his elder brother used to work as a high school teacher in the village, but now he is retired and lives on his pension.

Jack wanted to revisit the village to see his parents and see if he could convince them to move to the island. If his parents agree to migrate with him to the island, he will be more than happy to do so.

Jack bought many gifts for his parents and friends in the village before heading to the countryside. He knows his parents, brothers, sisters, relatives, and friends will be waiting for him and gifts.

While some friends would have sent to different places on the island, Jack did not meet with them. The island is big enough that they are lost and have never been together again.

When young people migrate to the island, they do not want to return to the countryside, they do not want to write anymore, and they do not want to be in touch with their families, but some of them would stay in touch with their families. In particular, Jack is the only one who always remembers his family and wants to see them.

ADVENTURE TWO

SOME YOUNG PEOPLE WHO LIVE IN THE COUNTRYSIDE HEARD ABOUT THE ADVENTURE ONE. They have been in touch with Jack on phone. Jack told them in detail about the standard of living on the island.

They were so excited to know that Jack entered the island. They were about ten people. They were all teenagers. They wanted to do the same adventure Jack did to enter the Fertile Island. They wanted to begin a new life. But they do not know how to do it. They looked for assistance from someone who knows authentic information about Fertile Island.

Once upon a time, there was a man in the countryside; The name of the man was Philip; he was sixty years, and he used to visit the island. He has been on more than five times on business to the island. He used to do business between the countryside and the island.

Someday, he went to a restaurant in the village for dinner with some friends. While waiting for his friends, one of the teenagers next to him asked for a tourist guide.

Philip questioned the boy the following questions:

"Why do you look for a tourist guide?" Philip inquired.

"We are ten teenagers who heard about the rich island, we wanted to go by land to the island, but a tourist guide seems important." Teen said.

"When I was younger, I went to the island more than ten times on business. I never used a boat to go there. I ride camels to go there. I was stronger and younger in time. The island is rich, and islanders are so kind." Philip explained.

"Would you be able to guide us to the island?" We are going to pay you a lot of money." A teenager said.

"Yes, I agreed to be a tourist guide and take you all to the island. I still remember the safe road that went to the island; the journey perhaps takes a month to be there." Philip said.

"Let me inform my friends and prepare ourselves and get back to you as soon as possible." A teenager commented.

A week later, they all got ready and met with Philip to begin their journey. They named it "adventure two" They had she-camel for the old man to ride and milk when they needed to drink milk during the long journey.

They started adventure two in the summer, and the weather was warm. They had enough food and drinking water for the journey; the teenagers were walking on foot while the tourist guide man was on she-camel.

They walk in the daytime and rest at night. They had a good time at the beginning of the journey. Sometimes they had severe forecasts and challenges in the middle of the sea, but all youth enjoyed traveling on the sea despite cloudy weather conditions and a lack of food and water.

Most of the teens were so excited to adventure and so comfortable with Mr. Philip made them so happy by telling short stories. He sometimes tells fear stories and likes to tell stories about Jinn and devils in the desert. They all laughed and enjoyed such fearful stories.

Philip acts as a storyteller to make the journey more enjoyable and successful. Some day at night, as they were resting and making food, they saw a glittering light in the sky.

They were wondering to see such a huge light. The light was slowly approaching them.

"Look at that light in the sky, they exclaimed.

"That light was made by devils to fear us and to move from here because we are sitting in their territory. You know, devils do not want a human to approach their territory, but do not worry, I will drive them away from here just for tonight and not to bother us," Philip remarked.

"How would you do that Philip?" Teenagers inquired.

"He went and milked she-camel, put some milk under small bushes near she-camel, and returned. After a few seconds, the light had gone away, and they all had asleep nothing happened to them all night.

Teenagers spent twenty days on their journey from road to road and from one hilly area to another, passing a small land full of flowers and trees. They came across a small village. They came across small deserted too.

They were lucky to find some date trees and picked a lot from them for their journey; some teenagers had injured their feet while walking in some hilly areas.

After twenty days, Mr. Philip "In the next morning, we will enter a small desert behind the island; it will take us a week to cross it and reach our destination."

He added "The desert is not so big, but if the weather gets worse and worse, it might take us more than a week to get into the seashore," they kept walking in the desert for three days, and suddenly the weather forecast changed and gets windy and dusty.

She camel would not walk, and Philip had become sick with fever and cough. He could not walk or talk. He died on the ground; they all became sad because their tourist guide had passed away in front of their eyes. No one knows to lead or help and guide them, and no compass to help them with directions.

They disagreed among themselves, disagreed about which way was the right one for the island, agreed to disagree, and disagreed about listening to one another to get to their destination, where they stood so close to their final destination was Fertile nation.

They separated into different groups and kept walking towards the island, where they lost their way to the island or maybe still walking towards the island.

Who knows?

Does nobody know?

Maybe there they are lost in the desert;

Maybe there they went to another place and live there.

Maybe there they are still wandering in the desert and do not know where to go.

Their families are waiting to hear from them.

If you hear about them let their families know.

MR. JAMES HEARD THAT the teenagers who traveled to the Fertile Island were lost in the desert. He had a small Jeep and wanted to search for them in the desert. James was familiar with all directions. He does know to live in a desert; he drove to the desert to find out if they are still alive.

MR.JAMES lives in the countryside where the teenagers used to live. He was surprised to hear the circumstances which caused them to wander in the desert. He is a very religious man; he believes in the Lord, says his prayers, and does a lot of supplication that the Almighty is helping him to get them alive.

He left the village in the morning, and at sunset, he was already in the middle of the desert. He stopped and made some food. He was always traveling with his old friend.

They spent all night at one place in the desert, and the weather was not so bad. They have enough food and drinking water. They also understand how to live in a desert or travel across the desert.

In the morning, they started looking for a trace or any sign that could help them to follow it. They did not see any remaining food for humans wandering in the desert.

At sunset, while they were about to stop and rest, they saw a small fire from so far. They decided to continue driving while they were approaching the fire. There they saw three men sitting around the fire. They laughed and sipped tea.

They arrived at the fireplace where the men welcomed them. They offered them some tea. They asked them if they needed help. They accepted the invitation and sat around the fire.

MR. JAMES explained the purpose of the trip to the desert; the gentlemen were shepherds of camels in the desert, and they were listening attentively to Mr. James.

They understand the story of the missing teenagers in the desert, one of the three men went to milk the she-camel to make porridge. The other two shepherds requested Mr. James to stay for tonight.

In the early morning, the desert is wet and not fair for walking and searching, they all begin walking in different directions, and they design a circle on the ground to meet again at the end of the day.

They began searching with their Jeep. Some of them used their camels as desert transportation. They spent all day searching from one place to another and failed to see any sign or trace of humans.

They all returned to their camp and spent another night. Consequently, a shepherd convinced them to be patient. They might find a trace or some remaining food somewhere if the weather stays quiet and calm.

The next morning, they began searching for some places in groups. One group separated to search for other locations. One shepherd shouted at the team and told them that one group saw several dead bodies in the desert, and even the -camel was also dead beside them.

One man told them while he was walking on foot to the camp; he came across dead bodies, and she-camel that looked like dry bodies from a not long time ago,

They asked him to show them the location of the dead bodies, and he went with them to the place where the missing boys were not so far from the camp, the dead bodies were about two miles from the living camp.

They went to the place in the center of the desert where they found ten deceased and a man dead near the camel. They checked their entire luggage and found all their documents. They buried all of them beside the camel and left for their camp.

On the third morning, Mr. James thanked all the shepherds for their help and support in finding these teenagers and left for the countryside, he spent two days driving day and night.

The next morning, he arrived at the village, and the villagers welcomed him with warm hospitality, he informed villagers that he found all the teenagers and a man dead in the middle of the desert; he buried all of them and brought their documents to their families as proof.

Chapter 12

THE SICK ISLAND

The small islands had become sick because of the spread of an unknown pandemic in the whole region. The pandemic killed a large number of islanders. The pandemic killed men much more than women. Most of the islanders died of a pandemic. No doctor knows the cause of the pandemic. The pandemic caused a large number of deaths across the region. All doctors in small islands raised questions to identify the cause of the unknown pandemic.

The governments in all islands declared that islanders were in an ordeal. They faced the ghost of death and uncertainty; they started studying the situation to stop the pandemic from killing islanders.

The world health organization (WHO) warned islanders of that difficult situation Doctors in different fields of science help resolve and shape the current situation and identify the name and medical treatment for a pandemic.

The island had good doctors working hard day and night to figure out the cause of the pandemic, it was a challenging moment for doctors to identify the cause and name of the pandemic within a few days, but they were working simultaneously with other working professionals to come to up with a clear cut answer.

One of the decisions is that the government took immediate measures and locked down the island from interaction with the world outside, and stopped all international flights to flat the curve of the pandemic.

What is the cause of the pandemic?

Infectious disease specialist doctors raised several questions. Many doctors devoted much of their time in different labs to identify even the name of the pandemic.

The pandemic spread in the air. It is a kind of transferable pandemic. The environment contaminated caused death; islanders got it from the air pollution and transferred it from one person to another.

The Queen Locked down the island to protect other islands, but unfortunately, the pandemic had already spread and was out of control.

Some infectious disease specialist doctors thought positively that the pandemic occurred during islanders' travel from island to island, but doctors were still unsure. They investigate and research with different infectious specialist doctors the appropriate answer.

Lisa was roaming with her bike on the island to ensure that islanders had enough food at their homes. She was delivering food door-to-door contacts. While she was delivering food door to door, she suddenly got the virus. She had been in the hospital for a month. She was in critical condition; she stopped eating food and drinking water. She died in the hospital.

A few months passed the Queen also got the pandemic because she was in touch with the communities on the island. Someday while addressing a meeting with her ministries, she fell –down on the ground. She was taken to the hospital for a week. She spent a week in the hospital and passed away.

Three days later, the general commander Mr. Ferdinand, and several soldiers got the pandemic. They died in the army hospital as well.

Three months have passed, and no infectious disease specialist doctor identifies the cause of the pandemic. Islanders become sick, but no doctor knows why islanders become sick.

No doctor knows how to make patients well.

Believe it or not, within three months of the onset of the pandemic, the island had lost more than a hundred thousand islanders, and the majority of them were elders who already had some chronic diseases.

A month later, one good doctor named Christine, she is an infectious disease specialist doctor had been devoting most of her time in the lab to learning about the pandemic. Obviously, she found out the cause of the pandemic and its name of it, after killing thousands and thousands of islanders in different places. The name of the pandemic was pestilence and it spreads in the air rapidly and it causes death to islanders.

The pestilence also had killed five other Queens on small islands and many more ordinary islanders. The news broke out and announced the tragedy of the sickness of the islands and the death toll of the five Queens.

Doctors on islands managed to find out medical treatment for the pestilence after the pestilence killed thousands and thousands of islanders.

The situation in the Fertile Island had become miserable because of the loss of the Queens and the general commander of the army Mr. Ferdinand.

ROSE TOOK OVER THE POSITION OF QUEEN OF THE FERTILE ISLAND. Rose nominated the commander of the Navy unit to become a general commander of the army, she also did some ministerial amendments, but the new ministerial reshuffles did not include Rebecca. As a result, islanders were not pleased with the new Queen Rose policy.

The doctors give islanders new instructions to follow to flat the curve of the pandemic. For instance, germs fall into the food from the air, and islanders require keeping all types of food or drinking in a fridge. They should wash their hands from time to time with soap and water. They need to avoid large congregations in small places, and they need to wear masks and take some medication to keep their immune system strong.

At the same time, it was a good opportunity for Rose who works for C.I.B to take over the throne of the Queen on the Fertile Island. It was also a very good

Islanders cautiously followed the doctor's instructions. They follow medical advice to flatten the curve. That was a challenging time for islanders in towns.

The opportunity is for the five beautiful ladies to work with Rose for the interest of the Great Island.

On the other hand, the king of Great Island was thrilled to watch all events happening. The king commented on the media on the Great Island "we soon were going to dominate and collaborate with others willingly or unwillingly." He added, "Our turn had come to grasp and smuggle natural resources from rich islands to our beloved land wealth."

Life slowly started getting to normal in the islands. Islanders were not welcoming the new Queens in their territories, they were gossiping with one another on buses, trains, and downtown. They chat in a humorous way about the changes in the region; they ask one another about their future.

Under these circumstances, to perceive the large number of death among elders, the elders who live in senior residences; they have had high professional nurses and doctors to take care of them, and even, they have become sick and died.

Some of young generations fled from the Fertile Island to the neighbouring islands to save their lives, but the pandemic had already spread there. Most of the youth survived and returned later to their home.

The pandemic was spreading in summer, and every place on the island had been affected. In summer, many green trees withered and died nothing to entice the eyes. Small cradles had dried up, and land cracked down into small pieces.

The pandemic was spreading in summer, and every place on the island had been affected. In summer, trees withered and died nothing to entice the eyes. Small cradles had dried up, and land cracked down into small pieces.

They do have air coolers in their homes, but because of the high temperature in the afternoon, the air coolers could not beat the heat. It was unbelievable to see some islanders dying from the heat. Islanders died from the heat because they do not accustom to hot weather.

Islanders had been facing two things happening together, the heat wave from one side and the pestilence from the other. Some islanders went to the seashore to spend some time there. While they were meeting and gathering there, the plague spread rapidly and killed large numbers on all islands.

The heat wave occurred in summer, and many trees withered and died. Agricultural land looked so harsh and coarse, and the soil cracked and did not hold water or green grass.

Many animals left the island for other places to get food and water. Small cradles had dried up and died, Islanders went groups after groups to the seashore to get some shades and cool water to beat the heat.

All international news has been talking about the heat wave on the islands, all countries warn their citizens not to go to islands, because of the heat.

What lies ahead?

The island looks gloomy and tranquil on a sunny day in April. People lost hope in the absence of their old Queen. The island has become sick. All homes, lands, and fields were becoming uninhabitable.

Under these circumstances, islanders decided to come together to build their land. They also agreed to walk downtown, to chant the following stanza:

To build the island we require time and primer
To build the island we should be strong and designer
To build the island we have to work hard in silence
To build the island we accept silence and resilience.

SOME DAY MORNING, DARK CLOUDS WERE PILING UP AS MOUNTAINS IN THE SKY OVER THE ISLAND, the clouds look very scary and got down close to the community buildings. Some islanders thought wrongly that the Lord get angry with them and now the punishment is on its way to the island.

But that assumption was not appropriate; the Lord is pleased with them. The Lord ordered cloudy rain to rain heavily on the island to sweep away the contaminated land from the pandemic and devils.

The rain started in the morning and stopped in the evening. Water spread in every dry stream, and the dead cradle back to life. Birds come back on trees. The gloomy trees bloom to life with different colors.

Islanders in holy places say their prayers and are grateful to the Lord. islands look very green after the rain; islanders keep broad smiles to attract one another mild,

Why do islanders keep a smile? They wanted to enjoy their new life without striving.

They used to struggle and survive,

But now they wanted to relax and pride.

After heavy rain, all sick islanders recovered from their pandemics and sickness. Some islanders believed that the Lord had sent rain, and it rains heavily on the island as a medical treatment for all sick islanders and lands.

After the rain stopped, the island changed for the better. Islanders smile broadly and talk happily to one another with great happiness and respect. The island becomes safe and secure from all illnesses.

The Queen invited islanders to a big party at the city hall for Thanksgiving, the new life, and the change on the island, the Queen provided islanders at the party with food and drinks to take away.

The artists in town had made two beautiful maps of the island; they built the two islands maps of marble:

One map represents the traffic movement filled with beauty and peace. The other one represents the time of the sickness of the land filled with ugly images of dry streams and rivers. They made the two marble maps as a historical event for the coming generation to learn about it.

The two pieces of the marble maps of the island are kept in the museum downtown for visitors to study and learn from them, they visit the museum regularly to know the history of the old nation in the island. While they were wondering in the museum, they found a marble map of the island that describes the lifestyle of the sick land because of the spread of the pestilence that killed thousands and thousands of islanders.

The museum becomes famous in the region due to the two pieces of the marble map of the island. The museum draws the attention of tourists regionally and internationally to visit. The museum was one of the most attractive places for tourists.

The government also spent a lot of funds to develop the museum and make it in good shape to attract visitors; there are more than fifty employees in different sections. It becomes a place of culture and heritage of the island in everything related to the historical background of the island.

Chapter 13

MAGISTRATE IN ISLAND

ONE EVENING ABOUT A YEAR AGO, the island had completely recovered from its sickness. Islanders felt confident to get back to their normal life. In the same year, islanders celebrated the New Year in the city hall, they all hope that the beginning of the New Year will bring, hope, success, and happiness for everyone.

Islanders had agreed to make a big celebration on the Fertile Island and invited all Queens and commanders from other islands into the city hall. They organized a unique festival that draws the attention of all islanders to come and participate in different activities.

The celebration had been continuing for three days in the downtown, city-hall with lots of food and desert, the celebration was supported by the government. There were a lot of islanders at the festival, some leaving, and some coming.

The city witnessed various programs for children. It was a busy place with different programs for kids to play. The kids liked the place and spend a lot of time playing games. The vast majorities of kids spend all day playing with one another and never grow tired of playing. They hate the time when their parents ask them to go home.

Adults had spent much time watching the cultural program that represents the folks of all islands. Adults come to celebrate and socialize with one another. They also met with new adults who come from other places to have fun in downtown.

One of the important things was the media channels that covered live celebrations downtown with all its activities worldwide. People come from all over the world to watch the festival and learn much from it.

While islanders in downtown, they saw fireworks in different colors as a rainbow in autumn. The only thing that draws attention is the children's afraid of the fireworks. Some children even cried out loud.

It was sad to see sometimes joy and fear occurring at the same time. Surprisingly, islanders enjoyed watching fireworks at the festival, while children were in fear of watching fireworks at the festival.

NEXT DAY ABOUT TEN O'CLOCK IN THE MORNING, THE RADIO OF THE ISLAND ANNOUNCED that a Supreme Court magistrate on the island had arrived. He was going to govern the island. But he was not going to be a good governor. Unfortunately, all the authoritative positions will be in his hand.

Queen Rose became a nominal executive while the magistrate was going to be the chief executive. Practically, that is part of the evil plans on the island.

Two hours later, the magistrate appeared on the TV Channel. He informed islanders that he was going to issue a set of decisions by tomorrow. He did not tell islanders the reasons that he was here and for how long will he be governed?

The next day morning, the magistrate issued a new order that restricts the movement of islanders between all islands, for instance, if an islander wants to travel to the other island, he or she should get a permission letter from the government service.

A week later, the magistrate treated all employees in the high court unrespect fully and arrested all activists; he also replaced all previous bills that protect the islanders' rights with a new bill that violated islanders' rights.

He controlled the movement of islanders from one island to another and from workplace to another. The implementation of the new rules turned the island into a big prison.

He went further and connected the places of the natural resources with a fast train-go and min-buses. That type of transportation helped shape the movement of islanders from homes to workplaces.

He trained a large number of islanders to drive truck lifts or cargo lifts and other necessary tools that would be required in the mines. The labor jobs have been kept for islanders.

If an islander refuses to go to work in the mines, the authority had the right to send him to jail. Many islanders had been sent to jail because they refused to compel.

The situation on the island was getting worse and worse; many islanders were becoming sick at work because of the unsafe work environment. Many islanders were becoming ill from overwork.

The work environment on the island made a large number of islanders had become diabetes and disabilities. There was no medical support from the government for those who had diabetes or disabilities.

The train started carrying islanders to work in the mines. The magistrate plans to work for the interest of the Great Island. The Great Island peacefully hijacked the wealth. The Great Island had placed Rose as an evil plan on the island.

Islanders worked in the mines for the interest of the Great Island. They were working with too low wages and had no benefits from their work in the mines. Additionally, they had no right to speak out for their rights. They have no right to leave the island somewhere without a permission letter from the service office.

The government did not allow ships to stay in the harbor when they were not traveling. The restriction is in all islands. In particular, commercial ships come from somewhere to the port with goods and other natural resources.

The island was surrounded by heavy security to keep all islanders in and not to allow them to leave their homes for another land.

The previous Queen kept the entire island's wealth in the palace; she informed islanders that she kept all wealth for islanders in the palace. She added, "That there were five big rooms in the palace packed up with gold."

One study showed that the only reserve of gold is in palace where could keep the island strong and survive for more than fifty years. The study confirmed that the island is thoroughly rich in natural resources.

The magistrate found an amount of gold in the palace. He constantly informed the king of the Great Island about it. The king gladly sent a commercial ship to the island to smuggle it.

A week later, the commercial ship arrived at the port, and the magistrate ordered islanders to come to the city hall and uploaded the multitude of trucks with gold in the palace.

Islanders did not know where trucks were going to drop that amount of gold; the drivers were foreigners working in the interest of the magistrate. They learn from Rose that the gold sends to the Great Island. They did not dare to tell islanders where trucks place the gold.

This plan was becoming an integral part of Rose's policy.

Rose works behind closed doors with the magistrate in collaboration with other Queens to take all natural resources to the Great Island.

Rose visits Queen's island to meet confidentially with other Queens. She keeps them sending reports to the king of the Great Island. She is responsible for following up in person to ensure the evil plan operates successfully.

Islanders do job laborers for the new governing system, and islanders enforced to work in the mines. They needed to work badly to bring food to the tables for their families. There was no more social assistance on the island; no more food bank or Salvation Aid that supports islanders.

Some islanders began to mutter and complain about the new governing system, but no one listens to their complaints, some islanders went further and wrote petitions to the magistrate but the magistrate does not respond.

Some islanders raised their voices and inquire:

WHAT THE HECK?
WHAT THE HELL?
WHAT WAS GOING ON HERE?
WHAT SHOULD WE DO?

The island is in ordeal and islanders are in terrible because of the new governing system. The magistrate is on the island showing no mercy.

The magistrate imposed a new bill encouraging all islanders to speak French; if an islander did not know French, the magistrate had the right to send him to French Schools.

Another island had imposed a new bill that administered all islanders to speak English, if an islander did not operate in English; the magistrate had the right to send him to English Schools.

In some other islands, the magistrate imposed the Italian language as an official language. If an islander does not speak the Italian language, the magistrate has the right to send him to Italian Schools.

Ten years have passed, and all young generations on the islands learned different languages, but the magistrate does not allow youth to go further in educational institutions. He needed the youth to master the languages and go to work in the mines.

Three companies were working in the mines, the French company, the Great Island Company, and the Italian company, a magistrate planned to train islanders in all languages before being sent to their workplaces.

The magistrate abused the governing system on the island. All natural resources of the islands had been smuggled and destroyed. All islanders have been living in poverty and depression.

"THERE IS ALWAYS A LIGHT IN THE TUNNEL"

The brave lady Rebecca managed to escape from the island to Denmark and began a campaign against the chaotic system on the island. Rebecca utilizes the space of freedom in Denmark and talks in several seminars and meetings in Denmark to draw the attention of the international public opinion to the miserable situation on the island.

The Regional and international organizations offer support to islanders suffering psychologically and mentally. The organizations approached the magistrate to remove restrictions on islanders. The magistrate turned the islands into a prison in which activists were tortured.

THE BRAVE LADY REBECCA managed to escape from the magistrate's control to Denmark to expose the magistrate's violations at all forms levels on the islands. Rebecca had been supported in that critical situation by all international organizations.

Rebecca gets help from some islanders who used to work with the previous Queen. They maintained the code to access all sensitive files of the governing system. They provided Rebecca with all criminal activities committed by the magistrate on the island.

They print all the documents that hold the account of the magistrate and the way the magistrate used to abuse the human rights on the island. They handed Rebecca a high-quality profile to bring the magistrate to the international criminal court (ICC) for justice.

Rebecca got the necessary information about the magistrate. She disguised herself in a security uniform and left through the main gate of the island because every person in the security thought that Rebecca was one of the members of the staff security.

Rebecca went to the seashore, where a small raft was waiting for her to escape. It was evening, the sun was going behind the hills, and it was nice weather and a quiet time to leave for Denmark.

Rebecca got into the boat and headed to Denmark. The weather was mild blows helped the boat progress on the water. She was sailing all night. In the morning, she arrived at a small harbour where a small ship waiting for passengers.

Rebecca recognized one passenger on the ship. A passenger whom she knows was also heading to Europe. Rebecca met with him in one of the meetings in the Denmark a month a year ago. The passenger whom she met on the ship was originally from the Great Island. She told him in brief about the current situation on the island.

Rebecca did not tell him that she escaped from the island and was now heading to Denmark. It was an unsafe moment to talk to passengers about the current situation on the island, the gentleman was curious to know about the current situation on the island, but Rebecca said: "I feel tired now, and I wanted to go for a little nap and talk to you later, she left him and went her room."

Rebecca did not show up for lunch, but she asked the waiter to bring her some snacks and mineral water to drink, she lives in her room to avoid interaction with people on the ship.

The journey took ten days from the island to Denmark. Rebecca arrived in Denmark in the early morning. In the afternoon, she went and met with the Queen of Denmark. Firstly, she met with the Queen's assistant and requested an appointment with the Queen.

At ten in the morning, Rebecca met with the Queen and explained the miserable situation on the island and how much islanders were suffering from the magistrate's policies.

Rebecca continued talking about the political situation in Fertile Island and what the magistrate had done to destroy the island and islanders in different ways. In the magistrate's time, the situation on the island was declining in every way.

Rebecca showed the Queen authentic documents proving that the magistrate abuses human rights on the island. The Queen understood the message and reacted immediately with other countries and international organizations to condemn that violation of human rights.

The international organizations held a meeting in Denmark and strongly condemned the current situation in the islands. Strong condemnation helped make the magistrate retreat from the islands after the exploitation of all the natural resources.

Rebecca confirms to the public that the king of the Great Island collaboration with the C.I.B behind that invasion and violation of human rights added: "The role of Denmark and international organizations function as a pressure group on the king to stop violating human rights.

Chapter 14

NAYA'S FAMILY
LEFT BEHIND

THE ISLAND LOOKS GRIEVED IN THE ABSENCE OF THE QUEEN NAYA. The families on the island have been in trouble under "a Supreme Court magistrate who took all teens from their families and sent them to the working camps.

The magistrate sends teens to work in the mines. He put them in different packaging sections at companies. They were packaging small pieces of gold in big boxes while elders uploaded heavy boxes on large trucks.

Trucks were lying up waiting for their turn to upload with gold, trucks were being uploaded and moved from the palace to the seashore where a ship ready to be uploaded.

Youth were suffering from hunger, they had no enough food at workplaces, they had little food per day, and they had paid a little wages too.

A number of elders were dying at work. They were dying from overwork; they had no clean drinking water and healthy food. Some of them died of illness because they did not have enough medical care, or medical insurance. The majority of them passed away through neglect.

Instead of sending little girls to school to be better wives in the future, they send them to mines to be gold diggers, to carry a heavy load of gold on their backs and upload it on trucks.

They have been starving while working in the mines.

They have been dying while detaining in the mines

They have been crying while remembering the earliest times

A lady was working hard in the mines. It was unbelievable to perceive a man over seventy workings in the mines; it was not acceptable to perceive a man of seventy working under the sun for long hours. Contrary, women trained to drive Forklift trucks to upload trucks. They have been working hard for ten hours and get paid a little wage.

So many institutions are closed. Not only colleges are closed, but also universities are closed. The magistrate allowed only elementary and secondary schools to remain open to help islanders to learn languages to communicate at workplaces.

The youth suffered during that time because of overwork, lack of rest, and water. Islanders were drinking water from the taps. Yes, of course, contaminated water caused sickness among workers. Intentionally, the government does not care about providing islanders with social services.

Some islanders had become mentally ill and died through negligence. No one could dare to ask the magistrate for protection. Some young generations started smoking marijuana at an early age. Some young generations began stealing because there they are lost, and they lost their memories.

It was unbelievable to perceive many islanders in rags cloth. It was miserable to see old islanders begging in the streets. It was frustrating to see some beggars in the downtown streets.

The magistrate does not care about them and even does not talk about them. The situation on the island during the magistrate era was getting worse and worse. He was working in the interest of the king of the Great Island. He does not listen to the islander's claims.

One such example is John's family moved from the countryside to the island for a better future? He was shocked to perceive such a miserable life on the island. John's wife Lucie had been sent to work in the mines instead of being sent to school. Lucie refused to work in the mines. The security guard arrested her and put her in jail. Many islanders were detained because they refused to work in the mines.

The security guards treated detainees in jail unfairly and made them live in dark rooms. The security guards do not allow them to see their relatives who come to visit. Most of the time, the security misleads islanders while visiting their siblings in jail. One such example is an islander who comes to visit his friend in prison, but the security guard told him that his friend already released, but in reality, his friend is still in detention.

John surprisingly lost if he could return to the countryside and raise his children there. He thought many times to leave the island where he was born. Yes, indeed, he used to work in the mines, and had a choice to raise his children the way he likes.

On the island, John had no freedom to raise his family as he wanted, but it was too late for him to fix that problem because the vast majority of islanders had been deprived of their rights by the dictator magistrate.

The problem that remains is the sickness of the land
The problem that remains is the sickness of the people

The problem that remains is the absence of justice
The problem that remains is the absence of decency
The problem that remains is the absence of integrity
The problem that remains is what lies next ahead.

REBECCA'S TURN HAS COME TO LEAD. REBECCA RETURNED FROM DENMARK TO THE FERTILE ISLAND AND BECOME THE LEADER OF THE ISLAND, she works closely in collaboration with other nations to help shape islanders in every way.

It was an uneasy task for Rebecca to heal the sickness of the land. Nonetheless, she never gives up and continues consulting many supporters in health and social services to assist islanders to heal from their illnesses.

Denmark quickly sent a medical team equipped with complete medical equipment to help patients of all levels. Denmark convinced international organizations to engage in providing humanitarian aid to islanders to get out of this ordeal.

Many international organizations are involved in supporting islanders with all necessary measures to overcome obstacles and difficulties that cause depression and sickness in islanders.

It took Rebecca ten years with the help of Denmark to make islanders return to their normal life and live with dignity and respect. She does a lot of positive changes in the ruling system to make islanders' life much better than ever.

While islands were glooming and prospering, the other parts of the world were declining and suffering, the Great Island was in ordeal, and the economic situation was in recession.

Rebecca requested international communities to send some specialist doctors in different fields to assist islanders suffering from depression and anxiety. Indeed, the communities react immediately to Rebecca's call and send teams of social workers to engage in the process of healing islanders from depression and anxiety.

While the magistrate was leaving the island, Rose was assassinated by an unknown group in the palace. TV News announced the assassination of Queen Rose, yet no one knows the cause behind the assassination. Nobody claimed responsibility for the event.

The Intelligence Office points the finger at the king for committing the crime, but the authorities on the Great Island denied that accusation. The situation on the island was becoming miserable, and every islander had enough to make him careless of others.

Someday evening at three o'clock, there were a group of people in black entered the palace and took the funeral of Rose somewhere.

The islands become empty of foreigners and business people. If you walk down the road downtown, you will see only islanders sitting in a circle and chanting of out out.

Rebecca understood the mode of islanders, and what had happened to them during the era of dictator magistrate, she started implementing a unique health care for all islanders. She succeeded in establishing a unique health care that provide all medical treatments.

Rebecca knew that it was not an easy task to resolve all problems within a day or night, she did well to make a lot of positive changes on the island. She opened universities, and colleges and hire qualified teachers and doctors in all fields.

Rebecca's brother John decided to stay on the island and help islanders to stand on their feet. John decided to do that paying back to the islanders who welcomed him when he needed them.

John also started to take care of elders in the community. He supported them with all types of things that they needed. Elders have nurses, food, storytellers, and a small theater to please them.

Rebecca opened jails and released all prisoners, and closed them forever. She claimed that our island does not need jail to detain innocent islanders, Rebecca added that "jail, in general, should be damaged and replace all of them with recreations places for islanders.

John met again with his wife Lucie who has been arrested in Jail for years. She lost her memory and she did not remember her husband John. The medical team comes from Denmark for help. The medical team approached and met in person with John and told him that they would like to treat Lucie.

John was pleased to meet with one of the best neurologists who promised John to make Lucie recover from her illness. After two weeks of medical treatment, Lucie started slowly to heal and remember things and even began recognizing her husband.

Lucie would not be able to heal completely and get back to life, but at least she knows things and communicating with her husband very well, John was happy to see his wife's health improved, he thanked the medical team for all their support.

John promised to stand with his wife in her ordeal and never leave her alone, and to devote much of his time to taking care of his wife.

John informed his sister Rebecca about his wife's situation, and his sister was glad to hear that Lucie had improved much more than ever before, and she was also glad to hear that John devoted his life to please his wife.

That was a good part of the marriage relationship, and that was an excellent dedication manner and obligation in terms of marriage certification, John took his wife every evening downtown to meet with her old girlfriends and have some social chat.

The island is rich with all natural resources; Rebecca worked harder to please islanders. She does that in order to make them forget the previous dark days.

She declared the island is a state of welfare and makes islanders live in a high standard of living. She offers islanders many benefits that allow them to live a well-being life.

Rebecca knows the importance of education and health care for islanders. She announces that education, medical treatment, and transportation will be free.

She opens more hospitals, schools, colleges, and universities for learners. She also allows international students to come study on the Fertile Island. She offers job opportunities for employees with high wages.

The island was becoming one of the best places in the world to live. All international organizations encourage other countries to look at the Fertile Island as a model and learn from it.

Rebecca made a great relationship with other countries based on mutual benefits and respect. The island had become well-known for wealth, justice, and decency.

Many countries around the world get benefits from the island in terms of humanitarian aid and business. The island has its doors open to help people who are in need. The island also supports all international communities in demonstrating peace and justice.

The island exports gold and natural gas to the world outside. Many international companies invest in the island, and some have collaborated with the island to exchange experiences in all different fields.

Chapter 15

THE KING OF THE GREAT ISLAND

The king of the Great Island was working with Rose behind closed doors. He was creating all types of problems on the island, particularly, the looted gold by the helicopter plane from the island. The king himself sent Rose to the Fertile Island to work for the interest of the Great Island, Rose sneaked slowly into the island and by hook and crook she succeeded in hacking the governing system of the island.

The Great Island was a superpower during that period. The Great Island is very rich too, but its richness occurred by invading other rich countries and looting their wealth.

The Great Island had become richer by smuggling gold from other rich places around the world; the king had a strong C.I.B on the island. The C.I.B developed and maintained to spy on other islands.

The C.I.B is working in the interest of the king of the Great Island. The C.I.B provides him with maps and locations of natural wealth on all islands. The king had a big army and the strongest government in the world.

The king is selfish and a dictator at the same time. He did whatever he can to control his people. He does not consult his cabinets for any serious actions; he was a bad ruler and dictator.

The king was focusing on Fertile Island because the island is very wealthy. The king studied the situation on the island through its C.I.B at all levels.

The king got what he was looking for on the island with the help of Rose and other assistants on other islands. The king started implementing his evil plan. The king sent the magistrate to rule the island and smuggle its wealth to the Great Island.

In ancient times, the king invaded some other countries and smuggled their natural resources to the Great Island. In time, the international organizations were not strong enough to condemn the policy of the Great Island.

In recent times, international organizations had become stronger enough and aware of the importance of justice and respect. Moreover, most of the countries in other parts of the world did not agree with the king of the Great Island in his aggressive plan. The perception of king of the Great Island was looking for a wealthy land to invade.

The new generation in all parts of the globe rejected the idea of invasion and smuggling wealth from other nations. The new generation believes in sharing wealth and that could be done by donation or business organization.

The new generation did not agree with the king's policy. They united as a young generation and form one strong body to protect their wealth from invasion.

One such example, the formation of the United Nations is to keep peace and security in all regions. The formation of the United Nations is to help to stop intervention.

Again, the king of the Great Island was planning to take action against the wealthy islands and control them.

He was planning to implement his evil plan, but in time, he was hesitant to march, he was afraid of international public opinion.

The king was searching for a partner in taking action against wealthy islands, but he did not find any other partner to share with him the evil plan. He was very aggressive toward other countries, but the unity of the other countries made him stop taking action against the island.

The previous king who ruled the Great Island was a good ruler. He respects the role of institutions and respects the role of the independent courts. He believes that the law is above all. He believes in justice and decency.

King Leer served as the 45th king of the Great Island. He was a bad ruler. He did not respect the laws and institutions on the Great Island; he did not respect correspondents in all his press conferences. He kept attacking some TV media and believed that some TV media tells lies. He says that in public conferences many times the media does not tell the truth.

When he came to power, his logo was making the Great Island great. The island is already great, but the king mentioned in all conferences that he was going to make the island great,

The king announced that he was planning to build a fence all-round the Great Island to protect outsiders from infiltrating the island. In time, all countries are opening their doors to help, inspire and learn from others.

The king treated correspondents in all press conferences unfairly and with disrespect. The king kept telling liars in the media and always tells liars in the media about many issues that concern islanders.

The king takes action without consulting his advisors. He was abusing the role of the legal authority. He neglected the separation of powers. He thought he was an expert in every way; he believed that all the executive and judicial authorities were in his hand.

People resented the king's internal policy of racial discrimination among the citizens. And he took measures to remove anyone against his conceptions in his internal policy.

All states on the island rose due to the king's extremist policies, and most of the islanders rose against him and demanded his removal from the government. The rich island was considered to function as a model of peace, love, dignity, and equity.

The king gave the green light to the security forces in the Great Island to disperse peaceful demonstrations in a number of states, and he threatened to take down the army on the city streets to oppress the demonstrators if necessary. Indeed, he ordered the deployment of the army in the cities of the island, and that was what the islanders upset with him.

In his last days of power, the king used his rhetoric and encouraged his followers to attack the symbol of peace and justice in town. He promised them to be there but he declined, he did not show up. He added "I encourage, I respect you, and you are somehow special to me"

The king's announcement made some islanders comment on it as follows:

"I tell you, the king is dangerous," the First islander said.

"I trust you now that I have heard him repeatedly ignited in his rhetoric," the Second islander commented.

"Why do not we islanders meet and throw him out of power?" The first islander claimed.

"Or impeach him," the Second islander agreed.

The king is playing with power." The first islander noted.

"I agreed with you." The second islander replied.

"Leer is corruption king, the first islander said.

"Yes, indeed, he was corrupted by absolute power, he did plunge the island into bloodshed and we witnessed the riots on the streets." The second islander affirmed.

"He abuses, power and fears his opposition, he loses the power he already has. Should we react or should we listen to this crazy king" the first islander asked?

The world was watching closely at the renewed violence across the island. All the high-ranking people of the world that respect the law and personal freedoms rejected acts of violence in all its names. The world nation looks with resentment and blames the king for igniting strife and hatred among islanders.

All dictatorial regimes throughout the world were watching and pleased with the violations of human rights on the island, which gives them a license to do more oppression and torture their citizens who stand up to speak out in public about the abuse of human rights in the Great Island.

The king turned a blind eye to the crime of killing activists. He did not condemn the illegal violations practiced by the dictatorial regimes against activists, and innocent people, and promise not to prosecute the criminals.

Unfortunately, the king was playing a negative role and let the enemies of freedom and democracy to carry out their acts of murder and abuse with every activist who stood up to injustice to silence him.

Islanders held fair and early elections in which the new candidate won the loudest vote. However, the king refused to acknowledge the defeat and launched a hostile campaign against the new elect king. He refused to leave the Golden Palace.

All election committees affirmed loyalty to the integrity of the elections. And all islanders know that the election is fair, and the king must go without his return. Indeed, the king has defiled the island's reputation in front of the world's opinion.

Eventually, the king left the government, and his country was suffering from the spread of the unknown pandemic that caused death to millions of lives, and the island has become at the forefront of the countries in the world affected by the unknown pandemic.

The king was planning to invade the Fertile Island and took all its wealth. He thought wrongly that he would be able to take action of invasion and smuggling the island wealth.

While he was planning to take action against the Fertile Island, islanders stepped out into the streets across the Great Island. Islanders were demonstrating and asking the king to step down because he was abusing his power.

The king found himself in a very critical situation, he could not able to take positive measures to fix the problems on the island, and he failed to convince islanders to stop demonstrations.

The unknown pandemic erupted all his plans and islanders died in thousand and thousand per day. He did not have any new strategies to combat the pandemic. He was only thinking of himself and how to be in power.

The king did not believe in science, doctors could not get an opportunity to work freely and place their plans to combat the unknown pandemic; all infectious disease specialist doctors in science were shocked to perceive the king rejected the facts of science.

The new king elects found great challenges on the negotiation table, for instance,

- returning the Great Island to its first course among the nations, building trust amongst islanders
- stopping systematic racism
- creating fair job opportunities
- combatting the unknown pandemic

- supporting the health care system
- cracking down the domestic extremism

The new king elects had the ability to fix all the problems in collaboration with all professional departments in the government. The first step he wanted to do is to flat down the curve of the unknown pandemic. He encouraged all islanders to wear a mask in public and in gatherings.

The good news at that time, islanders listen to the new king elects and wear masks at all times to flat the curve. The king also supports islanders financially to stay home for a while to avoid the spread of the unknown virus.

The virus is challenging doctors of the new and renewed pandemic every time from shape to shape.

The new king elects anti the idea of invasion, violation, discrimination, and humiliation, he believes in justice, decency, and mutual respect, and he believes in solving problems through negotiation tables.

Chapter 16

THE WORLD IS IN ORDEAL

The king of the Great Island was planning to invade the island and dominate. While he was planning to invade the Fertile Islands, the unknown pandemic broke out from somewhere and spread across the Great Island, small islands and the land of Asia, across Europe, oceans, seas, rivers, across Africa, it took no permission of transgressing the country's borders, it was spread everywhere.

The great island did not take immediate action to lock down its borders. The flights continued non-stop from the Great Island to all over the world. The situation on the island was becoming devastating and miserable.

The pandemic spread in all communities and the government failed to take serious action on time. The pandemic had killed large numbers of inhabitants; the whole hospital had become overcrowded with patients.

The spread of the unknown pandemic hinders the king of the Great Island to implement his evil plan. He becomes busy fighting against the new pandemic.

The new king elects were extremely busy working on flatting the curve of the virus that created lots of difficult challenges in the land where almost everything was shot down, because of the spread of pandemic.

Hospitals had become full of patients. The majority of patients died and there was no cure for that pandemic. If a person gets sick, he will be isolated from the community for a while. Some patients recovered during their isolation while some other suffered and passed away.

The infectious disease specialist doctors of the world had given it different names:

- THE RED PANDEMIC,
- THE KILLER PANDEMIC,
- THE BLUE PANDEMIC,
- THE INVISIBLE PANDEMIC,

The pandemic contaminated the air, and some people left their home- town for place where there was no pandemic, the moment they settle down in the new place from somewhere the pandemic broke out and killed a large number of people.

On November 22, 1888, Dr. Wuhan, the Director of the Scientific Research Centre (SRC) located about two miles from the center of the Great Island, received an unexpected phone -call from the new king elects.

"Wuhan, this is essential, the unknown pandemic had already spread on earth, it may come from space, or it may come from a lab, we do not really know yet what to do to save islanders, islanders had died in groups after groups, I wanted you to come over with your infectious disease specialist team and investigate," the king requested.

"Well, well, what is a pandemic?" Dr. Wuhan.

"I wish I knew, But I do not. That is for your team to investigate and find out, but my guess is this virus is manipulated in the lab somewhere," the king claimed.

"I doubt your assumption this virus is manipulated in the lab." Dr. Wuhan responded. He added, "We will see how the future brings to us."

Three days later, Wuhan and his infectious disease specialist doctors, taking every possible precaution against the pandemic and other dangers, including the recommendation of face covering, checked and tested everything that they found inside the SRC.

It was in fact a very dangerous pandemic. It seems to be that could be transmitted from human to human. It seems to be transmitted through touching, shaking hands or being closed to one another, obviously, the pandemic is invisible, and the team took a sample and looked at it in the microscope which makes small things look bigger. The team identified the shape of the pandemic in the SRC.

The infectious disease specialist doctors would know exactly where it had come from. They took some samples of it from human beings and animals and bring them back inside SRC for investigation.

"SRC laboratory, records, analyses, and dedicated everything, so that scientists could see where every component of the pandemic and how it does look like?

Wuhan said.

Another team also rang up Dr. Wuhan and informed him that they got some samples and wanted to check them in the lab.

"Well, well, we would better take them all back to the SRC and check their activities, weight, composition, and so on," Dr. Wuhan commented.

"Although there seem to be more than two types of pandemic development, it seems to be a very dangerous pandemic that we had never experienced before in our SRC Lab." His assistant said.

For weeks and weeks, scientists had been working on the samples of the pandemic, which were brought from human beings, animals, and the atmosphere.

They were worried about it; while the infectious disease team investigating the pandemic, a little mistake that happened by the lab technician allowed the pandemic spread rapidly all over the lab.

THE WORLD LOOKS FOR AN ANSWER!

On December 3th, 1888, the world's leaders, and vast majority of the world's greatest infectious disease specialist doctors were meeting together at the Denmark conference to discuss the crisis caused by the unknown pandemic.

"My country, the Great Island has suffered the most from the pandemic, the pandemic that killed millions and millions of people, but the pandemic is not only a threat to our country but also caused a threat to all inhabitants in this worldly life." Dr. Wuhan answered.

"People in all parts of the world are demanding a better life, a healthy life, a clean environment from air pollution, yet life in all countries on earth was becoming much more difficult," Assistant health commented.

"Our scientists and experts in science have addressed that in forty years from now the world will have become in much more crisis even if this strange pandemic did not exist," Chinese scientists addressed.

"We are here in a meeting to discuss and find an answer to the current pandemic and how to stop this pandemic from growth across the world." Japanese scientist said.

"What is the latest situation in the whole world?" Dr. Wuhan inquired.

"We have applied all the skills that we have, but we could not find a specific vaccine to destroy this pandemic from happening and spreading amongst people at large."

The new king elects added "I believe Dr. Dong Chew had something to share,"

"Sorry highness King elects, at present I am extremely surprised and have nothing to say" Dr. Dong Chew replied.

Like everybody at the meeting, the greatest Russian Dr. Metric seems to be worried and attempted, "We Russian had made some progress, we had developed a vaccine recently which seems to be effective in hindering the pandemic from spreading and might slow it down, but still people should continue wearing a mask, even after their vaccination.

"I do not get it, after vaccination we should keep wearing face masks" Chines scientists commented.

"This pandemic will stop when it touches North, South, East, and West on earth" The king of the Great Island commented.

"We are not quite sure, flights, Birds might carry it easily from continent to continent, We could observe that nowhere is safe now, in this case, we would say the pandemic is a universal one, we must unite and find an immediate solution to stop this pandemic form causing more death on earth. Dr. Wuhan replied.

"You are absolutely right, the pandemic is becoming a universal one and we would not like to see differences amongst us, we need to be united at this critical time and work together, it is time to take firm actions in collaboration with one another to combat the pandemic." Japanese scientists suggested.

"I am the type of person who is responsible for the big lab on the island; I have a great team who is working hard to develop a vaccine to combat this pandemic." An African scientist mentioned.

"Obviously, there are more than three kinds of a vaccine in the market now, in which one I believe, I do not know." Japanese scientists spoke.

"All scientists who specialize in infectious disease had been silent up to now, please come forward and help resolve to develop a vaccine that could crackdown this pandemic, of course, we do not know when and how. But we scientists believe that there is a scientist who could join our team at this difficult time and come up with effective vaccination."

French scientist commented.

"Dr. Chang wing, the world's greatest virus specialist,"

"Why is not he here?" One of the leaders asked.

"I know that Dr. Chang wing is a friend of mine, and we have been working together in the lab for years, now he has been working on important research that might be relevant to our current problem." An Assistant lab replied.

The new king elects of the Great Island stated "leaders, scientists, pandemic specialists and experts in this meeting, thank you so much for all your participations, we all agreed to work as one team to this proposal.

"We wish Dr. Chang was here," "Please report back to us as fast as possible —with an effective vaccine. If not possible, there would not be a healthy environment for the mankind on earth.

The king brought his speech with the following questions:

- Why did we call for this urgent meeting?
- Which country is suffering much more on earth?
- If the pandemic did not exist, would you think that there would be no problems?
- Did scientists, experts, and virus specialists make positive progress in a fighting pandemic?
- Did the pandemic touches the whole world or only reach some parts of the world?
- What did scientists decide?

On the other hand, Dr. Chang Wing virus specialist, and his old friend Dr. Mike Bing were working in the lab on Small Island somewhere in the corner of the earth. They have been working for years to develop a new vaccine, the lab was well-prepared and also they have been provided with all the requirements to help develop a new vaccine that could protect people on earth.

Of course, they get paid well to come out with that new vaccine. The two scientists were working day and night as a result; they had developed that safe vaccine.

"How long would such a pandemic remain effectively in the air?

"You know, we must develop a vaccine that must be effective and safe, we need to protect people on earth, but I know it is difficult to develop a vaccine that would remain forever, based on my own experience in science, we could develop one that would last for months on earth and would be easily distributed from country to country by air to save a life." Dr. Mike responded.

"Let us work on a new vaccine now and make it be most effective than the previous ones." Dr. Chang said.

"How do we do that?" Dr. Mike inquired.

"We need to develop a new vaccine and test it on animals to make sure that it is safe before bringing it out to the public at large, at the same time we should continue developing an effective vaccine that could cause damage to most of the virus in different parts of the world," Dr. Chang suggested.

"they developed it and distributed it on their own private plane from country to country and from continent to continent, when they landed on earth, they met with many people and scientists, they were met by a great number of people and interacted with them and let them take the vaccine and flew to another place and do the same," Dr. Chang said.

The pandemic broke out rapidly in many places. Official channels were simultaneously talked about it. Everybody was surprised to see how Pandemic spread easily from one place to another.

SCIENTISTS GOT VACCINES TO COMBAT PANDEMICS. Up to now, the pandemic killed more than twenty million and is still alive and kicking.

Scientists made a vaccine for those pandemics, different types of a vaccine in the market now, but the pandemic is still alive. At the same time, the vast majority of the people around the globe were not quite sure if that vaccine is protecting them from the pandemic.

Scientists still recommended patients to take vaccine, wear a mask and keep social distance.

On the other hand, people were expecting to take the vaccine and to drop off the mask and interact with one another, but that could not be approved by doctors at that point, some people would like to take a vaccine that allows them to drop off wearing a mask, but people were still uncertain if the vaccine would work or not.

The vast majority of people died in thousands and then in millions and still the number of deaths is toll increasing on earth. The pandemic challenges virus disease specialists to come up with a strong vaccine that could convince people and protects them from getting it.

That type of dangerous pandemic made all Great Islands; great countries struggle to fight against pandemic. They failed in every way to take it under control.

A strange pandemic challenges the Great Islands and forced people in all parts of the world to cancel their trips, flights, and business, the situation gets worse and worse every day.

Scientists were working day and night in their labs to figure out what to do to control that invisible pandemic. Scientists were puzzled by the changing of the pandemic.

The pandemic forced people to wear a mask while walking in the streets, shops, stores, and Malls, the sick environment changed the feature of a person, a person must wear a mask in public transportation.

SCIENTISTS SAY: THAT PART-TWO- WAS THE SECOND WAVE. THEY DO NOT KNOW WHAT THE SECOND WAVE LOOKS LIKE.

THE WORLD IS IN AN ORDEAL

THE WORLD IS IN DISORDER

THE WORLD IS IN A DILEMMA

MAYBE TOMORROW WE ARE GOING TO HEAR ABOUT THE THIRD WAVE.

WHO KNOWS?

REALLY THE WORLD IS IN A REAL CHALLENGE AND WE DO NOT KNOW WHAT DOES HOPE PROMISE FOR THE FUTURE?

THE MORE DETAIL WILL BE DEMONSTRATED IN THE NEXT BOOK.

Book Two

The world is in the ordeal

Many years ago, people all over the world live in peace. They do have some problems here and there but they were manageable. The world is full of optimistic news as well as is full of pessimistic news.

A life motivated people to go work to feed their families. A life motivated students to go to school to build their future. A life motivated farmers to work on their farms to grow vegetables. A life motivated doctors to work in their fields to make people well.

Yes, indeed, people work in different fields; each person is being responsible for a different piece of work. They all combined to make us live in peace and love.

People contributed to social life and built communities to live in dignity. People in communities helped one another in terms of education and food production to avoid poverty, starvation, and humiliation, communities live in contented and sustainable development.

A long time ago, the social interaction between people on earth was very limited, yet they meet, and traveled on business, but it was happening in different ways and traditionally.

The world in the 18th century was looking differently from today in all walks of life. Yes, indeed, we do have a lot of difficult challenges and problems, but life is still looking so pretty and sweaty.

The majority of people would prefer to live in rural areas and contributes to green land and agriculture. Others would prefer to live in urban dwellings.

A part of world is not in good shape. In particular, the rural areas are still lack of agricultural equipment. Vast people in that part have little access to advance tools to be used in cultivation and production plan.

so-called great countries in the world, in time, have little interest in investing in some part of the dark world, due to some kind of diseases such as malaria and fever, just to name a few. People who live in that dark part of the world failed to some degree, to improve their countries in terms of Agriculture and industrial development,

Many rich places become weak in their relationship and interaction with other nations. They do not come to a general agreement that could help them to exchange their perception and ideas in all walks of life.

In this situation, most of these places remain undeveloped and backward for several reasons, socially, economically, and politically. It is very sad deep to see some people live on rich land with all types of natural resources, but they were not being utilized yet, due to the lack of expert people and vision.

They do have a connection with people outside in terms of business, education, and international relations, but they do not have a wide range of positive visions that can be implemented to build their infrastructures such as roads, highways, and sustainable development in municipalities.

Some people said a dark part of the world is rich but is in trouble from one angle. But some of them believe that is now in ordeal but promotable and attractable for all types of investment.

People still do many good things to promote it in every way but, that was not enough, people need to do much more in all walks of life to develop the places where they live and work.

People contribute to the development of many other places in terms of work and better life,

Many educated people migrated from one place to another help to contribute to societies, at the same time; they make good money to help their families back home. But, most of them never come back, in this case, most places of the world prepare, educate their people and let them move away from the land and that was a loss another way round.

People of Africa started cutting down a large number of trees and moved in by building huge sectors of businesses to attract customers to buy and engaged in such activities. The small places have been growing more than ever before and are occupied by new generations who think of better lives and ignored the idea of keeping the environment clean.

Some great manufacturing companies moved to A dark part of the world looking for investment and help to create job opportunities. In the meantime, some people do not aware of the importance of keeping their living places and working places decent and clean.

There is no actual reform in all parts of communities in different parts of the world, yes, indeed, some people wanted to demonstrate justice among communities but they fail to do so.

Why did they fail to do so?

Few people give the right answer.

Some people worked hard to do some changes for the future but they still need to do much more. People on earth have the responsibility and accountability to do well and be nice to one another. They must think of their living environment and work environment, but the majority of them do not care about their living environment and work to be neat and tidy.

Many parts of the world are still in full of natural resources, but the process of development is very slow due to many factors.

One such example: The ruling system in some places unfortunately does not allow the country to grow and develop. The governing system of the place would love to see its people suffer and live in poverty and ignorance, the governing system would love to take over and control the natural resources.

Some people have left their values and become selfish and greedy. Nobody likes to help and share the wealth with others; the big problem in these places is the ruling system that does not believe in freedom of rights and constitutions.

It seemed to be difficult for people in many place of the world to eradicate this type of dictator from its roots and replace it with a governing system that believes in constitutions,

The rich island is a new fertile land that drew the attention of all inhabitants to think of it and to move into it, and get many benefits from it; the other continents have been suffering from disease, lack of resources and job opportunities.

Could you believe it?

The end of the world is coming; many problems are happening, and non-stopping and natural disaster is erupting. There is no effective resolution to the current evolution. The land, the sea, and oceans are filled with the nation, but the smart generation is studying space exploration.

The current investigation from the infectious disease specialists, develop vaccination to please all nations, but they are still so far behind vaccination.

They have determination to continue developing an effective vaccination that could protect generation. Unknown pandemic spreads rapidly and fears nations. Unknown pandemic challenges science and education.

The world is in ordeal as long as a pandemic kills and no deal,
The world is in ordeal as long as hatred in human being
The world is in ordeal as long as no guarantee vaccine

Activities

AFTER READING

Did you enjoy reading this book?

Would you recommend an audio-book for adults to listen?

Why Rose is an evil plan?

Why many people leave their countries for another place?

Do you agree that the world is in ordeal?

Do you agree there is no better place than a home?

What would you prefer to live in a country or town?

The human being causes damage to the world:

A-Yes

B-No

Why so called great islands abuse the small islands?

Do you agree with the author that great islands have double standard in politics?

Do you agree that the abuse of human rights is still alive and kicking?

Do you believe that the realistic fiction occurred or conceivably occur?

Do you like this realistic fiction?

What should we do to make people live in peace?

Why cry the rich island?

Why the rich land is broken?

Who broke the rich land?

Do you agree that if there is no organization, civilization, cooperation and justice everything is breaking?

What does pandemic mean?

Do you agree that war is pandemic?

Do you agree that a Dictator is pandemic?

Do you agree that injustice is pandemic?

Do you agree that abuse of human rights is pandemic?

Do you agree with the author that pandemic may have had lasting impact on human beings?

Do you believe the world is coming to an end because of the war activities in differ parts of the world?

The infectious disease specialist doctors of the world had given it different names:

- THE RED PANDEMIC,
- THE KILLER PANDEMIC,

THE BLUE PANDEMIC,
THE INVISIBLE PANDEMIC,

"The five ladies have already formed their plan into five committees, each committee is composed of five persons, and each committee represents a country and its language. Each committee is sent to a different small island to run a business."

The problem that remains is the sickness of the land

The problem that remains is the sickness of the people

The problem that remains is the absence of justice

The problem that remains is the absence of decency

The problem that remains is the absence of integrity
The problem that remains is what lies next ahead.

Dear daughter Rebecca,
House No 25

The countryside, the village,
25/8/53

My name is Lisa, I used to be the Queen of the fertile Island, now I am retired but I am still active doing some other social activities in the communities at large.

I have had the experience of talking with a lady here on the Fertile Island, the lady whom you met in the graveyard; she is one of our working people in the mission. The lady told us about your difficult situation and how much you were suffering. She told us that you have had missed your parents when you were a little girl;

You did remember your parents, your parents are always in your heart, your parents are alive in your eyes, you keep remembering them, and you keep visiting them in the graveyard every Saturday, that gives you peace and comfort.

We decided now is the time for action to reward you as a great woman in our mission by inviting you to be one of our islanders, therefore, we requested you to come quickly to the Fertile Island. Come to the city hall, Fertile-Island, and there we will be giving you some advice,

we will be giving you free accommodation, and
free bus transportation, where the expenditure
will not be important.

Many greetings
Lisa, previous Queen of the Island

Oh, island with followers and trees
Oh, island with dignity and treats
Oh, island with love and peace
Oh, island welcomes Rebecca, please.

Printed in the United States
by Baker & Taylor Publisher Services